Take the Reins

Siobhan Muir

ISBN: 0692408886
ISBN-13: 978-0692408889

DEDICATION

Dedicated to all the Schumacher women, Helen, Beth, Kate, and JES. Thank you for your love, encouragement in writing, and for being strong role models. Bethany gets her strength from you, even when faced with a fantasy world.

ACKNOWLEDGMENTS

Writing a book is never really a one person job. In fact, it takes a great deal of hard work, editing, and research on the part of the author to get things correct. Great thanks go to Silver James who made sure my military references were right on and the typo bugs weren't too big. Thanks to Emily Yenawine for making sure my verbiage wasn't verbose and my grammar was clear. Thanks to Cara Michaels for helping me work out the Greek mythology and for designing the most glorious cover art.

CHAPTER ONE

Bethany Stanton viciously kicked the loose stones on the trail while her sorrel horse Killian ambled along beside her. She wanted to scream and hurl the rocks, but she had too much respect for her equine companion to act rashly. Instead, her hands fisted on the reins.

"Damn him!"

Killian tossed his head at her outburst and she patted his neck. It wasn't his fault her father was a controlling, arrogant bastard. Wearing the title of US Senator meant a lot in this country, but it didn't allow him to dictate who she'd marry. Or announce it. *Dammit, the Middle Ages when men sold off women for land are supposed to be in the past.* Apparently her father had forgotten his knowledge of history.

"If the damn fool thinks I'm just going to accept his choice in fiancé, he's got another think comin'." Even allowing the thoughts to pass through her mind ignited her fury more. "How dare he, Killian? Why does he think he can force that choice on me? It's the twenty-first century for God's sake."

Bethany tied Killian to a maple at the edge of the clearing to keep from jerking on his head in her rage. The

1

open space ahead of them always filled her with peace and renewal, but today the usually gentle energy of the glade seemed as unsettled as her own. Bethany had often retreated to this spot on her father's estate when she'd needed time to think, not knowing what treasures resided here.

She'd even fired off an email to her brother, Chief Petty Officer and Navy SEAL sniper Kevin Stanton, but he hadn't answered by the time she left for her ride. *Probably off saving the world again.* It wasn't fair to condemn him for that, but she needed her older brother's counsel, dammit.

Her gaze slid over the recently cleared land, scanning the ancient archaeological site they'd found a few weeks earlier. Bright pink flagging waved from posts driven into the ground in a grid pattern, marring the lovely symmetry of the ruins. Golden evening sunshine slanted through the trees, painting black shadows beneath the ancient stones set in a rough hexagon.

Hell, this site meant more to the pretentious bastard than she did. She was just chattel, a bargaining chip to wave at Daddy's competitors and possible allies. Just like her mother. Bethany's anger crystallized inside her chest. Eloise Stanton had been a trophy, an arm ornament, and a broodmare for all her father paid attention to her.

"You're an asshole!" Bethany wanted to scream it at his face and nearly had when dear old dad informed —*informed!*—her she'd be marrying his sycophantic protégé John Coolidge. John had stood there behind her father's right shoulder and smiled smugly as if the deal was done. As if she had no say.

"Fucking bastards, all y'all!"

She ducked under the flagging and she swore her rage actually sparkled in the air. She'd laughed in his face until her father told her invitations to the wedding had already been sent out. The date set coincided with the election in a little over a month.

Despair gnawed at the edges of her awareness. If she didn't go through with his plans, he'd sell Killian to a quarter horse breeder out west for a tidy profit, a breeder whose name she hadn't been able to determine. In addition, he'd turn her out. What could she do? Agreeing to his plans was out of the question, but she couldn't sell Killian and she didn't have a job to fall back on while in vet school. *The best revenge would be to disappear.*

Bethany had never run from anything in her life. Not that she'd get far. A sitting senator's prize daughter didn't just disappear. He'd have the Alphabet Agencies after her faster than anyone could spell FBI. *I guess it helps that he's on several of those secret government committees.*

Bethany stopped in the center of the site on a slightly raised hexagonal stone and dropped her gaze to her feet, trying to find a way out. *I'm too young to get married.* She grimaced at the memory of her grandmother telling her no good girl waited until she'd become a spinster. *Thirty isn't spinsterhood.* Besides, her father's choices of men tended to be those who'd benefit him, not her. *Hell, I don't even get the chance to love anyone before I'm tied down.*

The stone beneath her feet glowed softly in the fading evening light and Bethany frowned, crouching to get a better look. Swirls of sparkles, like faerie dust, puffed out of the central stone, filling the air with flashing illumination. Bethany jerked her head up as the glittering light coalesced and flowed along grooved lines on the floor from each corner of the dig, engulfing her in its radiance.

What the—

The wind kicked up, whirling the brilliance around her like a cyclone. Bethany dropped to her butt and threw her hands over her eyes, ducking her head. The rush of air stole her breath and dried her throat, rising to a screaming pitch. A whinny hit her ears and she remembered Killian tied outside the circle.

3

Oh, God, Killian! She tried to open her eyes and crawl for the edge of the site, but the air currents buffeted her, holding her in the center. Dust and glitter clogged her nose and she coughed around the scents of horse, fresh cut grass, and...*Honeysuckle?*

Blowing dirt whirled in a choking dance just beyond her toes and she hunkered down, coughing harder. She hoped Killian survived the strange dust storm as she covered her nose and mouth with the tails of her shirt. The wind howled around her, flinging stinging particles against her skin.

Bethany ducked her head as she rubbed the sight back into her bedazzled eyes. Wracking coughs rattled her chest from all the swirling debris in the air. Voices, some chanting, some—*whinnying?*—rose in a crescendo and her hacking added a treble beat to the cacophony.

Then something popped and the wind died down. Bethany's coughs slowed and she prayed she'd be able to breathe clean air soon. Her eyes watered with all the dust, but she raised her head and scrubbed her face, hoping to clear her vision.

The archaeological site sparkled around her like the dying remnants of a fireworks display. Through the foggy air and flickering lights, she caught movement. Several large bodies shifted fluidly, as if she'd encountered an entire herd of wild horses. The chanting had changed into shouts of surprise and anger.

Aw hell, that sounds serious.

Squinting against the dust, she searched for a place to hide. Where had all the horses come from? Had her father actually sent the *cavalry* after her? To hell with that. Bethany crawled toward the maple where she'd left Killian, hoping the dirt and dust would obscure her identity. If she could get to her horse, she'd blend in with the others and no one would notice her riding away.

Protecting her eyes from flying debris, she scanned the sky looking for the spreading branches of the maple above the cloudy air. She scrambled the last few feet, searching for the only horse legs not moving. She'd almost reached the edge of the site when a pair of striped hooves stopped in front of her.

Bethany froze and looked up, way, way up, into the scowling face of a fierce man. Wait, how'd she miss the horse's head? The butt of a spear hit the ground before her hands and she jerked back, falling to her ass again. So much for being a lady. Her mother would've been appalled.

The dust cleared a little more and she got a good look at the man mounted before her. Except he wasn't mounted. The horse's shoulders and chest sprouted from where his human legs should be, and the spot where his man parts should hang...

"Oh lordy, I don't think I'm in Kentucky anymore."

The centaur's scowl only deepened. He bent at what would be a human waist, leaning on his spear and stuck his nose no more than six inches from hers.

"What are you?"

Bethany gaped at the bearded face before her. She hadn't expected his voice to be so musical or smooth when coupled with such a harsh visage. "I..."

"What are you? Druid? Gorgon?"

Bethany drew back. "Wait, what? No, I'm human."

Deep brown eyes scanned her face, the scowl never leaving his features. "Humans are a myth."

The words were so absurd, Bethany laughed. "I've stepped into the Twilight Zone."

He snorted just like a horse would and straightened. "I do not know what that is or what you are, but you should not be here. Get up."

Bethany scrambled to her feet and glanced over the centaur's—shoulder? Back?—toward the maple, hoping to find Killian unharmed. If she could just get to him she might be able to get away. But while four-legged creatures filled the archaeological site, none of them sported a "simple" horse head.

Jeez, it's like the leftovers from The Godfather.

"Where's my horse?"

"Horse?"

She bit back a sarcastic comment about four legged creatures with real heads. "Yes, my horse. I left him tied to that tree."

"Tied?" Anger threaded through his voice and a meaty hand wrapped around her arm. "You tied someone to a tree?"

"Yes, I tied him." Bethany tried to shrug off his hand, but his fingers only tightened. "I did it to keep him safe so he wouldn't hurt himself during all the excitement of whatever you've been doing." She scanned the grounds again, but Killian was gone. Bethany swung back to the centaur. "What did you do with him?"

"I assure you, nothing has been done to your horse—such creatures are as mythological as humans." The centaur grabbed her arm and jerked her close. "You will come with me and the Council will decide what manner of creature you are."

"No." Bethany lifted her chin and faced the man down. She'd had enough of overbearing men telling her how things would be. "If I'm the mythological beast here, you can make the effort to be polite. You don't understand what I am? Fantastic, I feel the same about you. But I can tell you right now that manhandling me and dragging me off to God-knows-where will not win you any points, mister."

"You will come with me or you will be hogtied and carried."

"Not today." She used her nails to pinch the skin at his wrist like she'd done to her older brother when they were kids.

He yelped and released her. Bethany scrambled out of reach and bolted for the trees. She'd never outrun him, but she bet dollars to doughnuts they couldn't climb. *Yay for being related to apes!* She dodged the bigger bodies, and shot for the nearest tree trunk. Leaping for the lowest branch, she prayed her grip would hold and no one caught her ankles.

Shouts and hoof beats clattered after her as her hands grasped the bark and she dragged herself up into the leafy canopy. She'd reached the second set of branches when an angry squeal made her turn and her gaze fixed on the wicked barb of a notched arrow.

"You will get down now."

"No." Bethany shook her head.

"You will come down or I will shoot you down. Any questions?"

Bethany swallowed bile. "Not at the moment, no." The arrow head followed her progress back to the forest floor and never wavered. "All right. I'm down. Put the bow away. You're making me nervous."

The centaur frowned harder, but lowered his bow. "Will you come peacefully or do you need to be bound and carried?"

Bethany scanned the forbidding faces of the horse-men around her and hugged herself. "I'll walk, thanks."

"Very well. Do not try to run. You will be caught and then the choice of being bound will be made."

Yeah, I bet you'd like that, wouldn't you, big boy? She nodded and followed where he directed, out of the clearing with the odd stones. While they resembled the ones in her father's estate, these looked well-tended and used. *I'm not in Kentucky anymore, that's for damn sure.* The question was, how had she gotten to wherever *here* was?

CHAPTER TWO

Major Stephen "Mack" McMacken stood at parade rest while he stared at the man behind a large mahogany desk. "I'm sorry, sir. Can you repeat that?"

"I want you and your team to investigate the disappearance of my daughter, Bethany." Senator James William Stanton of Kentucky met Mack's gaze with utter conviction. His lackey, John Coolidge, stood to one side and nodded vigorously.

"Isn't this a job for the FBI rather than the Army, sir?"

The senator didn't quite sneer, but his lip twitched and his chin rose. "If I had any confidence in the FBI or their ability to tackle this problem, Major, I'd have called them. But the uniqueness of this event necessitates the use of a far more capable force."

Mack digested the enigmatic statement and tried to ignore the sinking feeling in his gut. As part of the Army's Supernatural Anomalies Investigative Field Unit or SNAIFU, it was his job to investigate the weird events encountered by the military. *And one damn letter off from SNAFU which is where we find ourselves most of the time.*

"Are you saying there's something abnormal going on with your daughter, Senator?"

"I wouldn't say abnormal—"

"Yes." Stanton didn't flinch as he cut off his protégé's hedging response.

Coolidge could be the poster child for Yes Men International. He reeked of smarmy charm and weaselly support. Mack kept his expression from curling into a scowl from sheer willpower.

"I see. Why do you think that, sir?"

Stanton opened his mouth to say more when someone knocked at the door and pushed it open.

"Excuse me, sir." An older woman hesitated on the threshold, her expression troubled.

Senator Stanton glared at his secretary. "What is it, Rosalie? Can't you see I'm in the middle of a debriefing?"

"Yes, sir. I'm sorry, sir." She held up a creamy note folded in half. "But it's something I thought you needed to see immediately."

Stanton gestured for the note impatiently, but turned his attention back to Mack. "Recent discoveries on my estate suggest there's more going on than a simple case of Bethany running away. Originally, I thought she'd left the estate by conventional means, but my security guards had no record of her leaving by the front gate." Stanton paused, nodded, and waved at the secretary. "Thank you, Rosalie. That will be all."

"Yes, sir." The secretary scurried out of the office and closed the door behind her. The senator didn't even watch her leave.

"It's been nearly three days, and since she didn't run crying to any of her less appropriate friends, I assume something else has happened. It wasn't until this morning I was informed she'd taken her horse as she is known to do when in a fit of distemper." He glanced at his smarmy protégé. "She and John are to be married this year before the election and it's vital she's home in time."

Damn, can this guy be any more of an asshole?

9

"What about her horse?" John wore an expression of exaggerated concern.

Mack raised his eyebrows. "You didn't notice the horse was missing, sir?"

"Not until this morning, Major. But I figured she'd just ridden out to 'find herself', or some such nonsense, and would be back when she got over it." The Senator waved a hand dismissively.

"If she's riding a horse, wouldn't she be easy to find with a simple search party, sir?" Mack tried to keep his voice even, but his derision seeped through.

"The horse returned to the stable alone, Major, just over six hours after she left." Coolidge shot an apologetic look at Stanton.

Mack shrugged. "So she set the horse lose and left on foot. Why would you need SNAIFU to look into it?"

Silence enveloped the office as the two political men exchanged looks. *Correction. Coolidge looked at Stanton.*

"That's need-to-know, Major, and currently, it's immaterial."

Mack nodded and mentally shrugged. "Okay, Senator. I don't think we can help you, sir. Please contact the FBI. I'm sure they'll have the resources you need."

He snapped off a quick salute and turned on his heel, heading for the door.

"You're under orders, Major." Stanton hadn't raised his voice, but he no longer sounded as sure as he'd been.

Mack paused at the threshold and gave the senator a solemn look. "Sir, while you are in charge of many committees in Washington and you have many ears in the powers-that-be, when it comes to the safety of myself and my team, I make the final decision about where we go and what we do. You say I don't need to know. If that's the case, you don't need my unit, you need the FBI. So, good evening to you and good luck."

Mack grasped the door knob and twisted, pulling the

door open. The senator sat in cold silence behind him, but Mack couldn't care less. He had men and women to protect, and one spoiled little rich girl in a huff and her arrogant father weren't enough to make him rush in half-cocked. *I'm not anyone's hero.* And he sure as hell wasn't anyone's lackey. *Nope, that's Coolidge's job.*

"Major McMacken."

Speak of the devil... Mack paused as Coolidge ran up, his face full of obsequious charm.

"Please, Major. We need your help. *I* need your help to find my fiancée." Coolidge added a veneer of *concerned lover* to his face. "She's been missing for three days and no one has seen her. We're desperate to find her."

"I hear that, Mr. Coolidge. But I'm not going to send my people in blind. If it's need-to-know, and I don't, then you don't need us. Contact the normal authorities to find your fiancée."

"We can't." Coolidge glanced around to be sure no one else overheard. Mack damn near rolled his eyes at the man's furtive motions. "Please come back into the office. I'll explain everything."

"No, Mr. Coolidge. That won't be necessary. We're done here."

"Please, Major, I beg you. Bethany isn't here...in this world."

Mack raised eyebrows. "We got multiple worlds now, Mr. Coolidge?"

Again, the smarmy man glanced around. "Come back to the office."

Despite Mack's better judgment, his curiosity prodded him to follow the wealthy weasel back to Stanton's office. Coolidge knocked and Stanton let him in, a satisfied smile curling his thin lips.

"I see you've come to your senses, Major."

"No, sir, I've come for explanations. If there really isn't one, then I'll be on my way. See, just like you, I have places to be and people to kill."

The senator gave him a flat look. "I've killed no one in my career, Major."

"That remains to be seen, Senator. You did say your daughter's missing and you won't give me the necessary information to find her. I'm thinkin' that's signing her death warrant."

Pink showed on the senator's cheeks as he glared at Mack, but Mack didn't care. Until he got the answers he needed, he wouldn't take SNAIFU anywhere near Bethany Stanton or the Stanton estate.

Coolidge cleared his throat. "Yes, well, we'd like to avoid that. Please, sir."

Mack didn't know which man he begged, but Stanton grimaced and shook his head first, morphing into the concerned father before Mack's eyes. "Very well, John."

But the look he gave Mack consisted of solid steel. "There's an old ruin here, Major. It's been around for years, but until recently, has been nothing but old stones and weeds." Stanton sat back in his chair. "The NSA detected strange energy emissions coming from the spot two weeks ago. When they sent researchers to discover the source, they found something straight out of a science-fiction novel."

Mack didn't move or blink. *Yeah, so?* He'd seen weirder shit than most sci-fi writers could come up with and he'd lived it. So far, this hadn't tripped his trigger.

"The NSA had only sent researchers posing as archaeologists a couple of days before my daughter went missing. Everyone had been told to stay clear, but when she gets her back up, there's no telling her anything."

Good for you, Ms. Stanton. "And her horse is missing as well, sir?"

"Yes. That's when we realized where Bethany had probably gone." Coolidge actually wrung his hands in theatrical worry.

"How do you know she went anywhere near this site?"

"Nearby searches turned up foot and hoof prints leading toward the old ruin," Coolidge said.

"Damn that girl! Why did she have to do this now?" Stanton crossed his arms over his chest.

"What can you tell me about the site that I can use to protect my own people?"

"Are you taking the job?" Stanton's expression showed satisfaction.

"Not until I have some idea what I'm dealing with. Your daughter has disappeared and you suspect your archaeological ruins to be the source of her disappearance." Mack shook his head. "But you haven't told me enough about the site to put my own people in jeopardy to go after her. What is the site, really?"

Stanton's fists clenched on his arms before relaxing. "We don't entirely know what it is, but preliminary reports call it a portal."

Mack raised his eyebrows. "A portal? Like a doorway leading...somewhere?"

"That's right, Major."

Ten years earlier, before Mack got assigned to lead SNAIFU, he would've laughed outright. But he'd lived and seen too much to dismiss the senator's claims. "Where does it lead?"

"That has yet to be determined. We were putting together an exploratory team when my daughter disappeared."

"And you're sure she stepped through this portal?"

"Where else could she have gone? There's been no sign of her." Coolidge paced the floor beside the big desk. "As soon as we found the horse had returned without her, we immediately began calling her friends. No one has seen her and her personal ID and phone were still in her rooms."

"The grooms found the horse with his reins snapped off." Stanton waved the note he'd received from his secretary.

"Do you suspect foul play here, Senator?"

"No, I initially suspected she'd been thrown when the horse spooked, but according to this, the saddle hadn't been disturbed." Stanton grimaced. "When we searched for her in her usual haunts over the last few days, we came up empty, and her car was still in the garage. But at least we have the horse back, so not a total loss."

Mack stood at parade rest, but he wanted to grab the Remington statue on the desk and throw it at the pompous bastard. "Why not a total loss, sir?"

"Bethany has a champion bloodline quarter horse stallion, sorrel in color, and goes by the name of Killian Ford's Tenpenny," John replied as Stanton sat back in his chair, rubbing his chin. "The loss to the breeding program of champion quarter horses would be substantial."

Jeez, no wonder Ms. Stanton wanted to get away. Hell, I've only been here for a half hour and I'd rather take on a nest of banshees than deal with these jackasses.

"Let me get this straight." Mack crossed his arms over his chest. "You're asking me to take my team through a suspected portal to an unknown world just because your daughter pitched a fit and ran away? A daughter you value less than a prized quarter horse stud. Is that the extent of it, sir?"

Senator Stanton's expression solidified into impassivity. "I'm not asking, Major."

And that should tell you everything you need to know about the sensitivity of the senator.

"Major, Bethany is very important to our plans." Coolidge's voice held pacification and Mack wanted to gag.

Not exactly high praise for Ms. Stanton.

"This is a matter of national security, Major." Stanton leaned his elbows on his desk, his expression tired. Mack didn't buy it for a moment. "We don't know where the portal leads or what's likely to come through it. We need to secure this portal, and your team has both the experience and the expertise to do so."

"And we need you to recover Bethany since it's most likely she's stepped through without knowing what it was." John spread his hands in helplessness.

"You didn't tell her what it was?" Mack raised an eyebrow.

"It was need-to-know."

Mack clenched his jaw. "Right. And she didn't." He swallowed a curse. "So this has become a search-and-rescue in the name of national security?"

"That's correct, Major." The senator nodded with satisfaction. "You should take Mr. Coolidge with you as he knows this estate and the portal site the best."

Silence enveloped the office and Mack did his best to show nothing in his expression. "I'm sorry, sir. Did you say take Mr. Coolidge with us on the mission?"

"Yes, that's right, Major."

Are you fucking kidding me? "Sir, my team is highly trained in the unusual and we work as a cohesive unit." He shot a look at the slick, perfectly tailored Coolidge. "You said it yourself, Senator. We don't know where the portal leads or what's on the other side. We can't have civilians to monitor while doing our jobs. While I'm sure Mr. Coolidge is capable"—*at selecting a tie*—"you brought in the best to secure the site and keep civilians safe. I cannot allow Mr. Coolidge to endanger himself in that way."

Mack refused to budge. There was no fucking way he'd babysit a yes-man just to satisfy a senator.

"You'll need him to show you the area."

"He can direct us and show us on a map, but I will not have him with the team, sir." *Take it or leave it, asshole. I'm not bringing your toady with us, and I'll walk if you insist.*

Senator Stanton stared him down, but Mack lifted his

chin and held his ground. The man must have heard the unspoken subtext because he clenched his jaw and nodded.

"Very well, Major." Stanton's expression remained stoic, but satisfaction curled through Mack at winning his case. Stanton held the reputation of a bulldog in the political sphere, but Mack didn't give a shit. His team, his rules.

"John, please take Major McMacken to the library and show him a map of the grounds. He'll need to be briefed on all the geography between the house and the site."

"Sir—"

"Just do it, Coolidge. We're running out of time."

The two men shared a significant look Mack couldn't interpret, and Coolidge nodded. "Yes, sir."

Good job, yes-man.

"Good luck on your mission, Major. And thank you for your help." Stanton stood and transformed into a silver-tongued politician, his perfect smile meant to charm and seduce. *Yeah, not working on me, jackass.*

"Yes, sir." He pivoted, not caring if Coolidge followed, and marched out the door.

This would be a clusterfuck no matter which way he looked at it, but at least he didn't have to babysit. Hopefully, they'd get in, grab the girl, and get out before they irritated whatever lived on the other side of the portal. Glancing over his shoulder at the yes-man, he hoped he didn't run into more of his ilk. *Please, God, let Ms. Stanton be less of a pain-in-the-ass civilian.* Given the men's description of her and the world she came from, Mack didn't have much hope.

CHAPTER THREE

Bethany hoofed it along the mossy forest floor fast enough to feel like a workout. *Hoofed it. Very funny.* The only ones with hooves were her forbidding companions. Despite their size and mass, their footfalls met with relative silence under the swaying branches of the trees. They kept a tight formation around her and they became more vigilant as they approached an odd glow coming through the trunks.

Fear trickled down her back and settled into the pit of her stomach as a lamp with a Tiffany stained glass shade came into view. What the heck was a random lamp doing way out here in the trees? Running water overrode the sounds of the breeze and the scent of damp earth filled her nose. Bethany stared in fascinated wonder as the centaurs led her past a dark stream chuckling over its mossy rocks. The single ornate lamp stood sentinel to the tinkling current along a path made of flattened, glossy stones worn smooth by the water's sculpting.

The big roan centaur noticed the direction of her gaze. "Take a lesson from her."

"From whom?" Bethany raised an eyebrow.

"She was once one of the Twelve Dancing Princesses. Surely even a mythical beast like you would have heard the story. They were once human, so it's said." He nodded to the lamp. "When they were derelict in their duty to the Archdruid of the Grove, they were turned into lamps, and stationed around the wood as a warning."

"Who's the Archdruid of the Grove?"

The centaur shot her a look full of disgust.

"What?"

"The Archdruid of the Dryad's Sacred Grove is the elder of all the trees. And he is not very forgiving after the loss of the queens."

"Who are the queens?"

He huffed an irritated sigh. "The Summer and Winter queens of the dryads."

"You mean the ones from legend?" Bethany shook her head. "I thought they were Fae."

"What do you know of the Fae?" The angry question startled her and she backed off a bit.

"Only what I read in books. You know, tall willowy people who use magic and mischief against mortals." She eyed him uncertainly. "The ones who come from Faerie."

He relaxed marginally. "You know nothing about the Fae, then. They are cruel and unpredictable. And they are the ones who caused the rifts in the world."

That didn't sound good and the sight of the princess lamp gave her the heebie jeebies. She hadn't come here on purpose. In the story, the princesses had defied their father, and evidently the Dryad's Garden, to visit here, but Bethany had stumbled across it by mistake. The centaurs wouldn't punish her for that, would they?

Looking into the stoic face of her escort, Bethany's hope drained away. Her gaze drifted up into the early evening sky, framed by pale white branches of dead trees. They looked like skeletal fingers desperately seeking sustenance. She shivered.

"This place is creepy."

"This is the Dryad's Garden. Do not stray from my

side."

"Why not?" Bethany crowded closer.

"The dryads' response will be swift and deadly."

"You mean, like the lamps?"

"No. I mean death. They do not take kindly to desecration of their lands." He scowled deeper.

"But you're here. Aren't hooves harder on the landscape than feet?"

"We've been given permission to be here. You don't exist."

"That's your fallback position, is it?"

He snorted, but said nothing.

Bethany eyed the trees with distaste and stretched her legs to keep up with the faster gait of the centaur beside her. There was no way in hell she'd stay in the creepy forest of the dead alone. *Where the heck am I?* Her fear and disorientation had numbed her assertive side for a while, but now her practicality crept forward and questions came with it.

She glanced up at the—man?—next to her and wondered how willing he'd be to answer. He looked like a tough customer with a heavy, scarred leather jerkin over his broad chest. A bow string crossed from his right shoulder to his left—hip? Shoulder?—and a quiver of arrow fletches poked up over his left human shoulder.

Only a centaur can have four shoulders.

The jerkin covered the junction of man with horse and she wondered if the skin just sprouted fur in a sharp line or if the transition flowed gradually.

And only a horse geek would be thinking about this now.

"Where are we going?" She tried to put a little distance between them now that the creepy white trees had fallen behind.

"To the Council of Elders."

His answers were as staccato as a Gatling gun. Small bursts of rapid information without much explanation.

Bethany tried again.

"What happened? How did I get here? This isn't Kentucky."

"I do not know 'kentukee'. You shouldn't be here."

"I know. You've said."

"I thought humans were myths."

You're the myth, buster. She stifled a giggle at the thought of the popular TV show. *Yeah, I'd like you to disprove this guy.*

"I'm real enough. My name is Bethany Stanton. And you are?"

She held out her hand to him to shake and he stared at her as if she'd offered him a snake.

"What?"

"I will not be enthralled by your magic, human. Until we determine your purpose here and your intent, you shall keep your hands to yourself."

Amazement slammed into Bethany so hard she stopped walking. The centaur's longer stride carried him swiftly beyond her and the others behind him parted around her like a rock in a stream. They halted, dropping their pike points toward her in a bristling cavalry pose, and Bethany's irritation mounted.

"What the hell are you talking about?" She slammed her hands to her hips. "What magic? I don't have any magic."

The leading centaur pivoted in a perfect dressage pirouette and she had the momentary fantasy of taking him into one of the local competitions to try out his paces. Raising her gaze to his expression, the fantasy died swiftly in the face of his deepening scowl.

Does he ever wear any other expression?

"Humans have destructive magic!" He thundered to a stop before her, the bronze rivets on his leather canon braces flashing in the light of his troops' torches. She held her ground. "Humans are monsters of legend, tearing the world asunder. Look what they did to the dryads."

20

"I don't see dryads standing as a lamp along a stream." She stared up into his blazing brown eyes, her hands on her hips. "*That* human was changed by magic of the dryads, not by any kind of innate magical ability."

"And if those humans hadn't failed the Archdruid, they wouldn't have been punished," he retorted.

"So they didn't do magic and the dryads used magic to punish them for using a magic they didn't have?"

His black brows lowered over his eyes. "Keep moving, *human.*"

"No." Bethany raised her chin.

His nostrils flared as he inhaled and she braced for a tirade. "I will not allow you to endanger the cohort with your delusional blather. You will move on if I have to impale you upon a pike and propel you. It makes no difference to me if you're injured or whole."

Bethany's fear returned as her gaze flew to the wicked points of the bristling weapons around her and the hard expressions on the men behind them. They'd do as their commander bid and she was the smallest horse in the herd, so-to-speak. Plus they each outweighed her by a good thousand pounds. *Headstrong* didn't even begin to describe them.

"Move."

The menace in his voice froze her blood, but she narrowed her eyes and marched past him with her head held high. *Order me around like a servant, will he? Bully. Just like my father and his sycophantic protégé.*

"May you rot in hell," she grumbled under her breath.

"Silence."

Sure thing, big boy. Bethany seethed as she stomped along what amounted to a game trail.

The leafy path gave way to hard-packed dirt as the trees gave way to meadow grasses. At first, the open space appeared small, but she realized she could only see grasses in the flickering light of the torches. No other features

21

loomed out of the dusky landscape.

The breeze rustling through the branches of the forest now cut through Bethany's light flannel shirt and tossed her ponytail over her shoulder. She shivered and rubbed her arms as the centaurs herded her across the grassy expanse. The sweet scent of crushed grass rose up from beneath their feet and she had the odd thought that anyone tracking her would only see a human's footprints leading a herd of horses.

Too bad they couldn't see that it's at knife-point.

Bethany estimated they walked for about a half hour in tense silence across rolling grassy plains before they reached what looked like an encampment of soldiers. A few buildings resembling barns crouched around the edges of the encampment and an open structure stood surrounded by deciduous trees. Steam billowed gently in the air, stirring the trees' branches. To the left stood a stockade made from tall sharpened stakes bound with vines. Men, for lack of a better word, patrolled the edges of the encampment armed with spears and bows. Some had the discipline not to stare at her as her escort brought her in, but a few off-duty men gawked and whispered when their commanders weren't looking.

Her escort stopped and Captain Crankypants sent one of his men off toward a larger barn to inform the general they'd arrived with a captive. Bethany scanned the faces of the locals in an effort to calm herself down, but the centaurs around her showed nothing but hostility. *Great. Alone with antagonistic men. This has not been my day.*

Eventually, the barn spit out several more centaurs. Most of these wore bandoliers of leather with colored crystals sewn into them, much like the "fruit salad" she'd seen on the chests of military men back home. Some wore beards or had heads full of white hair, but all were male and none had a happy smile. Bethany raised her chin and squared her shoulders as they advanced on her.

"Report, Captain."

The centaur who spoke crossed his arms over his ripped chest and scowled, reminding her of her captor. His horse coat could be described as chestnut with four white socks of varying lengths. The silver in the hair at his temples marked his age and sprinkled the clipped beard on his chin. *Wow, even here males do some primping.*

The captain thumped his chest with his fist and bowed his head in salute. "General, we discovered an anomaly while on patrol during the ceremony." He shifted sideways to display Bethany. "By her own admission, she's human, sir."

Murmurs erupted around her from the menagerie of elder male centaurs and the chestnut general scowled deeper.

"Human? It's not possible. They're a myth."

Bethany couldn't hold back a snort. "No more than centaurs."

"Silence." Her escort swiped at her, but she crouched and he missed.

"Back off, Captain. I've done nothing but cooperate with you. If this is how you treat prisoners, you have no honor." She stood out of reach and kept her gaze moving. She didn't want one of the others to grab her.

A rumbling snarl echoed from the captain's chest and his expression turned thunderous, but she stood her ground and prepared to dart under the centaurs if need be. These guys were big and fast, but sometimes small, quick, and smart could outwit them.

"Stand down, Captain." The general tilted his head and something shadowing a smile curled his lips as he gazed at Bethany. "Where did you find her?"

"In the ceremonial grounds, General."

"What were you doing there on this holy day, human?"

How did she answer that? "Taking a walk, sir. I didn't realize it was a holy day. And where I'm from, nothing was going on."

"Where you're from?"

"She said she came through the Rift, sir," the captain supplied.

Bethany gulped. "Rift?"

"The portal at the Guardian's Copse." The general nodded and his smile vanished. "Has it been thoroughly checked?"

"I left Corporal Tredon to oversee the final closing."

"No one else?" The general shot a look of disapproval to the captain.

"He runs alone, sir. He says it's for safety reasons."

"I would think today of all days he'd choose to have reinforcements. Send a small party back to him to be sure." The general raised his chin and the captain's shoulders slumped a little.

"Yes, sir. Teagin, Merryweather, head back to the ceremonial grounds and back up Tredon. Take three more men with you."

A chorus of "yes sirs" followed the captain's order, and hoof beats signaled their departure. Bethany couldn't see them around the other large horse-men penning her in.

"Any other anomalies, Captain?"

"No, sir. Just the one human."

"Very well. Leave her with me and take your company back out on patrol. I won't have any celebrants harmed upon their return from the Guardian's Copse."

The captain thumped his chest again, scowled at Bethany, and wheeled with his men to gallop back out of the encampment. She resisted the urge to stick her tongue out at his roan butt as he retreated.

"So, human, why have you come here?"

Bethany returned her gaze to the general and fought against a grimace. "I didn't mean to come here. As I told the captain, I was just going for a walk and I ended up here."

He tilted his head and strode around her, his gaze assessing, but not sexual. He waved one hand through the air behind the small of her back and grunted with surprise. "You're truly not a centaur."

"No, I'm not." Bethany narrowed her eyes.

"And not a gorgon or a druid?"

"No."

"Humph. We'll see about that." An appaloosa male sneered as he paced closer, striking out at Bethany's head to grab her hair.

She ducked and pivoted away from him, wishing she had a rope to hogtie his arms. Instead, she kept her gaze on the bigger beings, mentally calculating how fast she'd have to run to make it to something she could climb.

"Enough."

The general hadn't spoken loudly, but the authority in his voice stopped everyone in place. Bethany braced herself for evasive action, but held her ground. Men had been trying to railroad her for years and she'd hit her threshold of tolerance.

"You will be respectful of those in our village."

Bethany raised her chin. "Tell him that."

A smile quirked the general's lips. "It was a warning for him."

"Oh." Bethany grimaced. "Sorry."

The general grunted and turned his attention to the other centaurs. "I will take care of this disturbance and determine its danger to us, Stal Corbin."

The appaloosa man glowered, but nodded and led the other elder centaurs back toward the large barns. Bethany watched them go and reminded herself men with too much power appeared the same no matter the species. *They're just like dear ole daddy.* She didn't have much hope this general would be any different.

"Have you a name by which we can call you?" The general returned to stand in front of her.

"Bethany Stanton. From Kentucky." She refrained from holding out her hand to him.

"Greetings, Mare Bethany, I'm General Warrick Spearthrower." He gestured toward one of the smaller structures to the side. "Come with me and explain how you encountered the Rift through which you came."

She shook her head, but followed him. "Rift. Like a doorway between...dimensions?"

"I don't know this word *dimensions*, but I do know there are portals." General Warrick frowned in concentration. "I was just a yearling the last time there was any mention of humans in the world." He paused at the entrance of a small barn and ushered her inside. "Strange that you should appear today."

Bethany found herself in something like a cross between a sheik's tent and a college professor's office. Books and scrolls filled shelves bracing the walls of the room on either side of an odd U-shaped desk. Periodically she found an artifact of war—spearhead, arrow fletches, even a cavalry saber—but the office gave the impression of a scholar rather than a hard-core warrior.

"Didn't you say today was a holiday?" Bethany turned to face the general.

He eyed her thoughtfully and nodded.

"What do you call the places on either side of the portal?"

"Worlds."

Bethany shook her head. "Of course."

"If you know of these *dimensions* and portals, why did you step through one and not stay in your own world?"

"Because in my world they're fiction." Bethany threw her hands out from her sides. "They only exist in the imaginations of science fiction authors and storytellers. Hell, all y'all are straight out of a fairytale. Next you're gonna tell me there are gryphons and goblins I should watch out for."

The centaur shook his head. "The gryphons died out long ago and the goblins keep to themselves in their own kingdom."

"Right. Of course. What about dragons, werewolves, or vampires? Am I gonna find some o' them?" Might as well go for broke.

"No. The dragons chose to stay in the human world according to legend. And vampires are a human based species. Surely you've met a few?"

Bethany barked a laugh. "Not even close. They don't exist." She shook her head again. "Like you."

"I exist, I assure you."

Bethany resisted the temptation to poke him in his chestnut side just to make sure. "That's what I said to your captain when he claimed I was a myth."

"Perhaps you will then understand what danger you're in."

She rolled her eyes. "I don't, really. I haven't done anything, but I understand your men seem to wish me harm because they've never seen my species."

"As the captain said, you are an anomaly." The general settled his bulk behind the desk. "But perhaps your arrival is just what we've been praying for."

Bethany blinked. "Wait, what? You've been praying for a human to show up?"

He leveled her with a dry look, taking years off his face. "No, we've been praying for guidance from the Goddess, Epona."

"And you think I'm here to give it to you?" She gaped at Warrick. "How the heck am I supposed to 'guide' a troop of centaurs?"

"That's a very good question, Mare Bethany, and remains to be seen." He tilted his head and narrowed his eyes. "Tell me, had you a profession in your home world?"

Oh, lordy, how do I answer that? Professional arm candy for my politician dad?

27

"I was studying to be a vet." Might as well cash in on her dream.

The general blinked. "Studying to be a veteran? Have you fought many battles?"

Bethany snorted. "No, not veteran, veterinarian. It means I care for and heal animals. Particularly horses."

"So you planned to be a surgeon in your military?"

"No. I've had enough of military men to last a lifetime." They were only slightly better than political groupies trying to get into her father's good graces. "My father owns a stable of champion quarter horses. I'd hoped to become an expert in caring for them and their injuries."

"But you are female." He frowned and shook his head. "Is that not more of a male trade?"

Bite your tongue before you get speared, Beth. She lifted her chin. "My body shape and gender has nothing to with my abilities."

"I see." Warrick crossed his arms over his chest and dropped his chin. "So you know military men, horses, and, being female, how to talk to other females, yes?"

Warning bells went off in the back of her head, but she nodded slowly. "Yes, I guess."

"Let's do this. You shall speak to my Lead Mare about her recent recalcitrance, and that of the other mares in my harem, and I shall allow you to live unfettered in the village with our people."

"Wait. What?" Bethany gaped. "I don't understand. I have to talk to whom about what?"

"My Lead Mare, Idrissa Plainsrunner, the mother of my son, and the most stubborn female ever to gallop across the grasslands." Affection underlay his irritation. "She has been unhappy and I cannot find what it is to change this. So you shall do it for me."

Bethany ran through several questions in her mind before she settled on the easiest. "Have you thought about asking her what would make her happier?"

"Of course." He grimaced and looked away in a rare moment of vulnerability. "But she refuses to say anything of value. I do everything to secure her comfort, yet she spurns me."

Oh, terrific. I've landed in the middle of a domestic dispute.

"What do you think I can do?"

"I know not, but the Goddess wouldn't have sent you here without reason." His expression turned stony. "You will speak with her and get her to favor me again."

Bethany choked on the combination of amazement and indignation. *But I don't know anything about centaurs or marriage counseling.*

General Warrick strode from behind the desk and grasped her arm in an iron grip. Bethany stood so dumbfounded she didn't even protest until he'd hurried her out of his office.

"Wait, how am I supposed to get her to favor you? I don't know anything about you."

"You don't need to know anything about me. She knows." Warrick dragged her across the open space to another barn, this one with lovely scrolling details on the doors and eaves. "You are female and you can get her to see reason. Remind her of her place."

"Her place?" Bethany ripped her arm out of his grip and dug in her heels before the double doors. "You want me to tell her she should be a slave to your desires?"

"Of course. That's always a female's place."

Warrick yanked open the door and tossed Bethany, spitting with fury, through it. "Now, do as you're told." And he closed the door in her snarling face.

CHAPTER FOUR

Mack leaned over the maps on the grand oak table in the library with First Sergeant Circe Bryant and scowled. They had to be close to two hundred years old with scrolling along the edges and calligraphy naming the different landmarks on the estate. Ornate drawings filled the compass rose and the corners of the maps, depicting the wind directions.

"This is the most recent map you have of the estate?"

"Yes. They haven't needed to be updated because the estate hasn't changed that much." Coolidge pointed to what looked like a miniature compass rose in the middle of the map. "That's the site where the strange energy signatures come from. Nothing electronic works near there now."

"Now?" Bryant raised an elegant eyebrow. "Has that changed?"

Coolidge nodded. "The place has been a ruin. No one thought much about it until a Stealth pilot picked up some weird readings while doing a routine training run. We managed to shut down the scuttlebutt, but as soon as we could, we had folks out here to investigate."

"But you didn't tell Ms. Stanton." Mack couldn't hold back his derision.

"No, Major. Like I said, everyone avoided the place. There was no reason to tell anyone about it until we knew more."

"I'm thinking you're regretting that line of thought right about now." Bryant shook her head as she dragged her finger over the map. "How are you planning on going in, Major? Do you think we're going to be facing COUOs out there?"

"Coo-ohs?" Coolidge wrinkled his forehead, not the most attractive expression on a man with a large one.

"Creatures of Unusual Origins." Mack fixed Coolidge with a hard stare. "Will we?"

Coolidge swallowed hard. "There's an acronym for that?"

"Yep." Bryant clenched her jaw and Mack suspected she bit her tongue to avoid saying more. She didn't suffer fools. "So will we encounter anything odd out there?"

"No, Ms. Bryant. We haven't seen anything."

"It's Staff Sergeant Bryant, and how often have you been out to the site?"

"My apologies, Sergeant." Coolidge gave her a brief smile. "I've only been out there once."

And this was the guy I'm supposed to drag with me on this mission?

Mack forced the growl out of his voice. "Where did your intel on this site come from?"

"From the grounds keepers. They haven't reported anything unusual except their cell phones now won't work out there."

Mack shared a look with Bryant. "You verified we can't get close with electronics?"

"Yes, sir. All our usual toys stopped being accurate within three hundred yards."

Mack sighed. "It's gonna have to be line-of-sight the whole time, then, Sergeant. Make sure you reiterate that to the team." She nodded and he pointed back at the map. "I think we can follow the marked trail going in. If there's anything out there, we'll have a better chance of dealing with it out in the open than in terrain too thick for good visibility, especially without electronics."

Bryant nodded again. "Do we take these with us, sir?"

Mack shook his head. "No. They're too ornate to be much use and I have a photographic memory. Besides, once we get there, any maps we have will be obsolete."

"Yes, sir." Bryant pulled out a little notebook and drew a few lines.

"What are you doing, Sergeant?" Coolidge tried to get a good look.

"Drawing a map from this one."

"Why? I thought the Major has a photographic memory."

"He might, but I don't, and it's always good to have a backup." She sketched a few more lines and shoved the notebook into one of her pockets. "There are always things you wish you'd done when you hit the field. Not drawing a map won't be one of them this time."

Mack nodded. "Mr. Murphy often likes to screw with us. The less we assume we know, the better off we are." He stepped back from the table. "Let's get the squad together and head out. There's nothing more we need here."

"If you have any questions out in the field, don't hesitate to call me." Coolidge gave him an obsequious smile as he followed Mack out.

"Will do. Thank you, Mr. Coolidge."

Staff Sergeant Bryant leaned closer as the man retreated from them, her tone wry. "You mean with our cell phones that won't work out there?"

Mack snorted. "Yep."

They exited the mansion and headed for the stables, catching up with the rest of their crew. All eight people in his squad were damn good at what they did and never let him down. *And yet we're so screwed we're gonna need a*

32

DeWalt power drill to get us out of this.

"Major, we caught the farrier outside before he left. We're holding him until you can talk to him." Corporal Tillman had a head full of red hair and arched brows that gave him a perpetually surprised expression. Many a man had underestimated the corporal from his looks alone.

"Good job, Corporal. Bryant, debrief him and find out what he knows about Ms. Stanton's whereabouts the day she disappeared." Mack looked over his shoulder at the huge barn stretching into the late afternoon gloom. "I'm going to take a look in the barn and see if any of the staff knows more than Stanton is telling us. Something just doesn't add up here."

"Yes, sir. You want me to brief the squad about our gear?"

"Yes. No laser sights, no cell phones or GPS units, no flashlights. Nothing. Get our gear packed into the Humvees and lock them up. I don't need anyone without clearance getting a hold of anything." Bryant nodded and headed for the detained farrier.

Mack speared the corporal with his gaze. "Tillman, see if you can find any kerosene lanterns or, hell, candle lanterns in the barn or garden sheds around here. We're gonna need them."

"Yes, sir."

"I'll meet you back at the Humvees in twenty mikes."

"Yes, sir."

Mack entered the stable, listening for the horses shifting in their stalls, and spied a light doorway in the half-darkness. The scents of hay, manure, and leather brought back memories of home, but a new scent and the hiss of meat cooking popped his memory bubble like a pin.

The source of the smell sat in an old plush Laz-E-Boy in the corner of the tack room, his head bent over a tiny space heater held in his hands. Though he wore a sleeveless t-shirt, he was using the space heater to reheat day-old bacon.

"What are you doing?"

The young man jerked in surprise, then glowered. "Cookin'. What're you doin'?"

Mack bit back a smile. "I'm Major McMacken, looking for Ms. Bethany Stanton. Were you working the day she disappeared?"

"Shore nuff." He scratched under the edge of his backward ball cap. "She came in here all fired up and spittin' mad. Said she'd saddle her own horse, no need to be bothered. Once she had old Killian tacked up, she lit outta here like her ass was on fire. I ain't seen her so mad since her mama died."

"Do you know where she was headed?"

"Naw." The young man shook his head as he turned back to his reheating project. "She didn't say nothin' 'bout where she was going. But I know her favorite trail is the one that heads to them ruins everyone's goin' on about."

"Why is that her favorite?" Mack scanned the walls of the tack room, looking for any clue the old leather would tell him about Ms. Stanton's departure.

"I don't rightly know. But every time she came back from there, her anger was gone and she could face her daddy again."

I wonder if that would help me keep from shooting the slick bastard, too.

"I understand you found her horse."

"Yessir. Hiram brought Killian in and put 'im in his stall when we found him two nights ago. Fed him real good, too." The stable hand set aside his cooking apparatus and ambled out of the tack room toward the back of the barn. "Killian was all spooked and wouldn't settle down until we gave him some Sedalin paste."

Mack nodded as they passed several glossy heads poking out of stalls to investigate the newcomers. He knew about Sedalin. It was used as a mild sedative for horses undergoing surgery or other medical procedures.

"Here he is. Ms. Stanton's pride and joy." The groom's voice showed his own pleasure at the horse.

Mack noted the marks of the saddle on the horse's glossy sides, though he'd been brushed. "Where was he found?"

"On the same trail, only he was headed home at a pretty good clip accordin' to Hiram." He shook his head and leaned on the stall door as the horse rested with his head down and one foot cocked. "Reins were snapped off like he'd jerked himself free and he was blowing like he'd run the Kentucky Derby."

"Was there any sign of Ms. Stanton?" Mack studied the horse's relaxed expression. "Did the stirrups look pulled or torn? Any other damage to the tack beyond the broken reins?"

"No sir. Just them reins. Looked like she done tied him to somethin' and walked away." The stable hand frowned. "Then he spooked."

"Why did it take so long to find him? The senator said she's been gone over a day."

"We was told to stay away from that place even when they noticed she was gone." The stablehand scowled. "I ain't see them quite so twitchy about anything like this before, but those ruins give me the heebie-jeebies even from three hundred yards away."

"Did you find any injuries on the horse?" Mack tried to scan for wounds, but the darkness in the stall prevented a close inspection.

"Naw. He was fit as a fiddle. Just scared is all."

Mack nodded. "Keep an eye on him. If he does anything strange or out of character, report it. It might give us a clue what happened to Ms. Stanton."

"Right. Will do."

Mack followed the groom back toward the tack room, the scent of cooking bacon increasing with each step. As the young man ambled back to his comfortable seat, Mack smothered a grin.

"Why are you cooking bacon on a space heater instead of the microwave in the kitchen of the house?" He couldn't hold back his curiosity.

"The cook don't like us stable hands gettin' close to the house. She says we stink like horse shit even after we wash." He shrugged. "'Sokay with me. That woman's a harpy and smells like burnt oil." He wrinkled his nose. "Rather muck out stalls any day and twice on Sundays."

Mack chuckled and nodded. "Thanks for the information."

"Sure thing." The groom paused. "Hey Major?"

"Yes?"

"Find her and bring her home safe, okay? Ms. Stanton is the nicest lady in the family and don't deserve to have somethin' bad happen to her."

"We'll get the job done. I promise." Mack nodded again and headed back out to his squad. *Maybe she's not like her father.* If the staff liked her, there was hope for Ms. Stanton.

His path took him out to the Humvees where Corporal Tillman set out four lanterns of various sizes and fuels. They'd stripped the digital sights off their rifles and all their electronic equipment out of their pockets. The seats in the Humvee sat littered with flashlights, laser sights, cell phones and radios. Mack swore under his breath. He'd forgotten about the radios.

"Looks good, Tillman. Sidearms and knives should be okay." He scanned the other gear and shook his head. This couldn't end well with so much of their tech left behind.

"Thanks, sir. Should we pack the lanterns or light them?"

"Light them. We'll use them to get to the site."

"His name was Milo Scaggins." Bryant reported as she marched up, watching the farrier drive away.

"Are you kidding me?" Mack raised an eyebrow.

36

"Nope. That's the name he gave me in the interview."

"Milo Scaggins. Like a play on 'Bilbo Baggins'? Who would do that to their kid?" Mack shook his head. "Did he say anything useful?"

"Only that she saddled Killian right beside him shoeing another horse and rode off in a "big damn hurry." His words."

"Did he say which direction?"

"Same direction we're headed. Looks like she made a bee-line for the site."

Mack nodded and checked his weapons as he shouldered his pack. He hated being unprepared, but he didn't know what they'd find and each time they did this, it was something new. With all their high tech gadgets useless at the ruins, they definitely have to think outside the box when it came to this mission.

"That's convenient." He grimaced. "Was the horse newly shod?"

Bryant nodded. "Yeah. Why?"

"The tracks will be deeper and sharper. When horse shoes are new, they make clear depressions, especially if they have cleats."

"Horse shoes have cleats? Why?" Tillman lit a kerosene lantern, the low rumble filling the gaps between his words.

"Back in the day, it allowed carriage horses to have purchase, especially on icy cobblestone streets. Nowadays, they do it for polo ponies and tourist carriage horses." Mack grunted when Tillman handed him a lantern. "This all of them?"

"We could only find four," Tillman reported as he handed a second to Bryant.

"What, you couldn't run to Wally World?" Circe quipped.

"Dammit. We *will* need a DeWalt."

"A DeWalt, sir?" Tillman asked.

"To get us unscrewed, Corporal," Bryant explained as

she hefted the lantern.

"Get rid of your radio and cell phone, Bryant, and let's move out. We're burning time here and we don't know what Ms. Stanton is facing right now." Mack fitted a black knit hat snugly over his head and waved the rest of his squad to get moving.

Mack inspected each member of his team as they gathered and nodded to Bryant when he'd finished. No one said anything as they headed out into the Kentucky autumn night. A few crickets left over from the summer heat chirped slowly in the gathering gloom and a few of the bare-branched trees clacked together in the night breeze, but no other sounds disturbed the dark beyond their footsteps.

It took almost an hour of careful and quiet walking to get to the old ruins in the southeast corner of the Stanton estate, but Mack knew when they got close. The hair on his arms and neck rose in visceral awareness, and his nose tingled. He'd never tell anyone about the tingling—something about it didn't seem masculine—but it happened every time they approached a supernatural phenomenon. Mack raised his hand in a closed fist.

Taking a deep breath, Mack stilled and listened to the night sounds. A low hum reverberated in his breastbone and base of his ears, felt more than heard. Mack scanned the grounds he could see beyond the light of his lantern and everything looked quiet. *Yeah, looks can be deceiving in places like this.*

"Bryant, take a team and search the perimeter for more tracks." The team fanned out into the trees surrounding the ruins. Mack nodded to them and motioned he'd take point from the entrance as the lantern light spread around the archaeological site.

Mack dropped to his haunches to study the ground. The newest prints in the dust showed cowboy boots and horseshoes without cleats. The first set of horseshoes headed toward the site at average depth. The second set was deeper and spaced farther apart, showing an increased rate of departure. But no human boot prints came with them.

So she walked in with her horse, but the horse galloped out alone. Where did you go, Ms. Stanton? Mack picked his way closer to the paving stones on the floor of the dig, trying to avoid marring any of the tracks. The path opened up in front of him to show flagging the scientists had left after their survey.

He paused at the edge of the paving stones and inhaled. The scents of torches and incense wafted through the air, but the only light came from the lanterns bobbing in the trees beyond the site. The tingling returned to his nose and he gritted his teeth. The half-moon hadn't crested the trees yet, but sparkles, smaller than fireflies, drifted in the air beyond the flagging.

Mack shifted to the side and something cracked under his foot. He bent and set down his lantern as he grabbed an acorn with a frown. He scanned the leafy canopy overhead, recognizing maple, horse chestnut, and birch trees. But no oaks.

"What are you doing here, buddy? Where's your parent tree?"

Mack rose with the acorn still gripped in his fingers and surveyed the entire site. He squinted his eyes and wished he had his night goggles and radio.

Too bad the electromagnetic signature of this place futzes with them. He didn't need the equipment to tell him something energetically odd permeated this place.

The shadows danced in the flickering light of the lantern at his feet and he felt like some early explorer at the birth of the country, staring with misgivings at the night-darkened forest around him. He certainly didn't have the tech of a more modern society.

The soft hiss of someone moving through the

underbrush carried to his ears and he lifted his lantern to expand the reach of the light. Bryant wove her way through the trees, skirting the ruins.

"Report, Bryant. Found anything?" He kept his voice low despite their relative solitude.

"Yes, sir." She pulled out the old fashioned Geiger counter they'd modified to detect any portals they'd encountered over the years. Mack lifted the lantern to scan the analog read-out and swore.

"Yeah. Looks a lot like some of the midair rifts we found." She glanced at the flagging, a frown creasing her brow. "What I don't get is why the readings are so much lower here."

"I think it's because it's stable. Given the look of the place, sir, I suspect this one has been here a long time."

"That makes sense. Check this out." Bryant led him through some of the underbrush to the southwest corner of the circular stone paving and pointed to a carving in the rock.

Mack crouched to get a closer look. "Is that the Aztec double headed infinity snake you saw carved in that pylon at the edge of Angel Falls in Venezuela?"

"Yes, sir. And in the Giant's Graveyard on the Oregon coast."

"How the hell did it get all the way out here in Kentucky?" He scanned the site again as he rose to his feet.

"Think someone from the west coast stepped through one there and came back out here, sir?"

Mack stomach lurched. "Good question, Bryant. Here's a couple more. If that's the case, where do you go when you step through? Do they connect to each other or do they lead somewhere else entirely?"

"I don't know, sir. But from what tracks I could find, or rather didn't find, Ms. Stanton entered the ruins, but never came out." Bryant swung her arm and her gaze around the ruins. "There's no one else here but us, Mack. And the readings say there's a doorway. I suspect she stumbled across something she didn't expect."

Bryant's expression mirrored the sinking feeling in Mack's gut. "Fuck."

"Yeah."

They'd never crossed one of the doorways before. They'd always dealt with whatever crossed into their world. Things just got a whole lot more complicated.

"Are we going after her, sir?" Bryant's jaw clenched hard as she held his gaze.

Mack scanned the ruins and let the idea settle in his gut. Someone had to go after Ms. Stanton. She'd be even less prepared to deal with whatever lived on the other side of the doorway than them. She needed the team. *Some of us.*

"Yeah, but not all of us. I want the majority of the team to stay here and guard our back door. Just you and me will cross the doorway."

Bryant swore and Mack gave her a tight smile. "Yeah, I know. It's not ideal, but better to lose just two of us, than the whole team. Call 'em in and let's get this show on the road. We're running on borrowed time."

Bryant disappeared into the darkness to call in the rest of the team and Mack waited at the entrance to the clearing. The breeze ruffled the trees, sending the scents of burning pitch to his nose. He searched the area around him, but saw nothing resembling torches anywhere. He continued to listen and inhale, but the site remained outwardly serene.

In minutes, the team gathered around him and he took in their wary faces. They knew they'd hit some sort of roadblock and come up empty.

"We've hit a snag, gentlemen." Mack met every gaze. "Ms. Stanton appears to have stepped through one of those portals we've detected."

"Aw, shit." Franco spat on the ground. "What are we gonna do, sir?"

"Bryant and I are going to take point and go after her. I

want the rest of you to fan out and protect our tails. Bryant, hand me your map." Circe pulled out her hand-drawn map and Mack laid it on the ground in the light. "I need three pairs of two all around the perimeter of the site to secure anyone trying to get in or get out. We don't need any more surprises from this. From what I understand, nothing has come through, but that doesn't mean we'll stay that lucky."

He met their gazes again. "The footprints around here indicate Ms. Stanton went through the doorway and hasn't returned. This has become a search and rescue, but that doesn't mean we won't meet something weird. Keep your eyes and ears open. We're going to have to do this old school. No tech to help this time. Are we clear?"

"Sir, how long do we wait until we come in after you?" Tillman's grim face looked older than his twenty-five years.

"No one's coming in after us." Mack used as much authority as he could dig up.

"But, sir—"

"Look, the fewer people we lose to this place the better. First Sergeant Bryant and I will go through to find Ms. Stanton and bring her back. If we don't return within twenty-four, return to the estate and contact HQ for instructions. You're not to come in after us."

He pinned the men with his gaze. "Lieutenant Barnes, keep the team here until that time. Then retreat. That's an order. I have to assess the danger to the team as much as the danger to Ms. Stanton. We don't know yet what we're facing and I'd rather have fewer casualties than the whole team. Understood?"

Barnes looked like he wanted to tell Mack to fuck off, and in the past he'd done so out of the rest of the team's hearing. But tonight he just tightened his lips and nodded sharply. *That's because he knows I'm right about the possibility of not coming back.*

The chorus of "yes, sirs" bordered on insubordinate, but

Mack understood their lack of enthusiasm. They'd been a team for eight years and no one left any member behind. This order would stick in their craw if Mack and Bryant didn't come back with Ms. Stanton.

"Right. Let's get to it." He resettled his pack and sniffed the air. The torch scent remained despite the breeze.

"Do you really think this is a good idea, Mack?" Bryant checked her own gear as the other men faded into the trees around the ruins.

"Nope, but if you got any better ones, now's the time to speak up."

She grimaced and shook her head.

"Ready?"

"Nope. I'll follow you."

Mack stepped onto the path and followed the footprints into the clearing. Their boots thumped on the paving stones as the moon crested the trees, throwing their shadows across the granite. The tingling increased in Mack's nose and he rubbed it to keep from sneezing. Swirls of sparkles kicked up from their feet, glittering in the moonlight.

"Uh, Mack? I'm getting an increase in radiation fluctuations." Bryant's voice held caution.

The glittering light grew in brilliance until it drained into the grooves on the floor of the ruins and shot straight for them at the center of the site. The breeze stiffened, kicking up dust and debris as they closed on the center of the clearing. Mack put up a hand to save his eyes as Bryant shouted something, but the sound was lost in the rising wind.

"I think the doorway's opening. Stay with me, Bryant." He raised his voice to carry over the wind, but he had no idea if she'd heard as the eye of the storm centered over them. Mack reached for Bryant, but the wind knocked him off balance and he stumbled backward across the center block of the site.

"Bryant!"

Dust and debris filled his throat until he coughed, his eyes watering from the foggy air. Mack staggered toward the outer edge of the ruins and something popped like he'd changed elevation. The wind died as quickly as it had risen and he rubbed his eyes to clear his vision.

His sight cleared slowly as the glitter faded from the air and the grooves in the floor. The moon hung higher above the trees, but the light seemed damn near golden instead of cool white. He coughed and scanned the forest around him. More lights than the lanterns from his men shone through the trunks. The scents of incense and burning pitch grew stronger, and shadows shifted beneath the trees with unsettling motions as if something large moved within the forest. The hair on the back of Mack's neck rose and he melted into the trees opposite the movement.

Mack dropped into a crouch and slowed his breathing in an effort to listen. Whatever moved on the other side of the clearing in the golden light of the moon spoke in terse commands and rough voices. The scent of burning pitch came from the torches they carried aloft. He couldn't catch any words, but the cadence sounded military, and they appeared to be mounted. *Fan-fucking-tastic. An unknown cavalry is all we need.*

He wished they carried their radios, but the energy of the clearing still raised the hair on his neck. He scanned the empty stones through the trees, searching for Bryant, but the only movement came from the retreating military group.

Where had his sergeant gone? She'd been right behind Mack when the wind kicked up.

Staying well back within the treeline, Mack worked his way around the clearing. Instead of ruins, the site appeared well maintained with no weeds or rampant growth around the main portion of the stones. Mack paused and listened for his NCO. The night breeze rattled the branches of the trees and the thunder of hooves rumbled in the distance.

Mack listened for a human predator, but nothing came to his ears.

Dammit, Bryant. Where the hell are you?

CHAPTER FIVE

Bethany stood at the large double doors of the barn and fumed. She'd heard no lock thrown, but with the size of the guards outside, they likely didn't need one. Reminding herself she needed to calm down to outthink this, she forced her breathing to slow and closed her eyes. *I won't let them beat me at this game.*

Once she calmed enough not to scream, Bethany turned to scan the surprisingly elegant space. Scents of sweet hay and gardenia flowers filled the air, and gentle breezes ruffled the gauzy curtains over the open windows. *Maybe I could get out through one of them.* Torches burned in sconces evenly spaced along the walls and the flickering light disguised the other person in the room until she spoke.

"What are you?"

Bethany jumped and met a pair of angry, steel-blue eyes. *Diplomacy, Beth. Remember it.*

She shoved back her snarky response. "I'm human."

The female centaur stepped closer, a frown creasing her brow. While her face remained unlined, crow's feet at the edges of her eyes marked her experience. A circlet of gold rested in her hair portraying her status as lead mare to the general's harem.

"To what do I owe the dubious honor of your presence, human? Have I angered the general so much he sends me a mythical beast?"

The smooth, feminine voice dripped with sarcasm, and a matching scowl conveyed her disdain. *Lordy, now I have a bitch of a woman to deal with. Bless her heart.*

Bethany gritted her teeth. "Trust me, Lead Mare. If the idiots outside would let me, I'd be gone in a heartbeat."

Okay, not the most diplomatic, but certainly honest.

"Do you insult us, human?" Her nostrils flared and she rested her hand on a wicked dagger belted to her human waist.

Deep breath. You're on her turf.

"No, I'm not insulting you, I'm merely pointing out I've been harassed, bullied, herded, and threatened enough today, thank you." Bethany crossed her arms. "The general suggested I reason with you, but it's looking less and less likely that I can."

The Lead Mare's chin came up and her hand tightened on the dagger's hilt. "Speak with respect, human. You owe me that."

"I owe you nothing." Bethany matched the woman's snarl. "I don't want to be here and I certainly didn't beg to be dragged here by your general."

"I suppose he thinks I shall give up my demands if he sends you as a gift." The Lead Mare raised her chin. "It won't work. I won't bend. The mares want to be heard and our requests are not without merit."

Bethany crossed her arms over her chest. "Have you tried telling him that?"

"Of course we have. But males only seem to respond to force, and this is the only way to force his attention." The woman narrowed her eyes. "You think we're simpletons who have done nothing to convey our desires? That can't be further from the truth."

"No, I didn't mean that." Bethany sighed and rubbed her

forehead with one hand. "Can we start over? I feel like I've stepped into a fantasy novel."

The woman's scowl melted into bitter laughter and her hand dropped from her dagger. "This is the real world, human."

Bethany glowered. "If you'd asked me this morning what the real world was, I would've told you there's no such thing as centaurs."

"Oh, yes?" The Lead Mare tossed her charcoal gray braid over her shoulder and strode to a crystal pitcher full of water. "Here, you are the mythical creature." She poured some water into a glass and sipped from it. "I thought humans were only legends my granddam told us to keep us from defying the Lead Stallion. Yet, here you stand in my stable. I suppose I should be properly reverent, but I'm finding it difficult to bow to such an insignificant creature."

Bethany's anger surged, but she gritted her teeth again and swallowed her words. *At least I'm not wearing a horse's ass.* Not very politic and certainly wouldn't improve her situation. *Breathe and remember your political manners.*

"Honey, if I wanted bowing and scraping, I would've worn my tiara." She crossed her arms over her chest. "I don't want your reverence, I just want to go home. Maybe you can convince the general that I'm not a threat to your people, and have no influence at all."

The Lead Mare's brows lowered and her frown returned. "I cannot even convince him to hear me out. How will I convince him of what you say?"

Bethany's gut sank. "Oh." She eyed the other woman thoughtfully. "So I'm supposed to change your mind to his way of thinking and get you to give up your demands of change?" She snorted and shook her head. "Boy, did he ask the wrong person to do that for him. I wouldn't agree to it at home, I'm certainly not gonna agree to it here." She scrubbed her face with her hands and sighed. "In fact, I'm having almost the same problems at home. Only, they're trying to tell me who to..." She glanced at her centaur companion. "Mate with."

The Lead Mare tipped her head and smirked. "And this is different from me, how?"

Bethany blinked. "The males tell you to whom you'll mate? Really?"

The other woman shrugged, but her lips tightened in frustration. "It is the way it is."

Bethany snorted. "If I was as strong as you, I'd fight it."

"Believe me, you would not."

"Oh, yes, I would. Different species or not, we're still people with a voice and an opinion. And I'll tell you this much. The women in my world fought for their privileges and won." She shrugged again. "Well, mostly. There are still some things we have to work out, like equal pay for equal work. But we're making headway."

The centaur woman tipped her head, her charcoal braid falling over one full breast. "I suppose it was easy for you."

"No, it wasn't. It took almost fifty years just to get a vote in our villages. And even now we fight for each foothold of change. But it's worth the effort." Bethany strode toward her and held out her hand. "My name's Bethany Stanton."

The Lead Mare stared at her hand as if it consisted of an odd shape and texture, but slowly reached out to grasp Bethany's thumb in her fist. Bethany closed her hand around the Mare's thumb and shook gently.

"I am Idrissa Plainsrunner, Lead Mare of the Forest Edge clan."

"Very pleased to meet you, Idrissa." Bethany released her and stood back. "The general shoved me in here to tell you to shape up, but I'm thinking he's the one who needs to change. I take it you've made it clear you're done meekly submitting to their orders?"

Idrissa snorted in disgust. "For all the good it has done."

"I think it's done something. He sent me in here in hopes it would soften you up. The thing is, the men only get away with it because women are agreeable. If you want it to change, stop being agreeable." *I should start practicing what I preach.* "I admit it won't be easy and it might be damn scary, but change only happens when it hurts bad enough." *So when am I going to stop being agreeable?*

"What do you know of the mating practices of centaurs?" Idrissa's expression filled with disdain again.

"Not a damn thing." Bethany shook her head. "But I know about people, and if a man wants to keep his woman, and keep her happy, he better treat her with respect. It's what I'd want from my man." *Not that I have one other than my father's stooge.*

Coolidge would be another version of her father. James Stanton had married into her mother's wealthy family to add to his inheritance, and once he had a ring on her finger, she became just another possession he'd accumulated for his political career. He took her presence as guaranteed and Bethany watched her mother slowly die emotionally over their thirty-year marriage, until she died for real.

I refuse to do the same damn thing.

"It is not a mare's place to tell a stallion that." Idrissa's voice held resignation.

Bethany snorted. "How else is he gonna learn it, then? If they don't get taught or told, they don't get it." She grimaced. "You have to give the stallion a reason to change. He won't change his behavior until you make it clear it's no longer working for him to get what he wants."

"He would punish us." Idrissa's anger gave a hard edge to her voice. "Do you not think we've tried this?"

"Have you really put it to the test?" When Idrissa snorted with derision, Bethany added, "Okay, you have. But I'm telling you it does work." She frowned. "Of course, I don't know centaurs. Can he be reasoned with?"

Idrissa snorted. "Rarely."

"Yeah. Human men are a lot like that, too."

"And what do you do to get better treatment?"

Bethany thought of her overbearing father and his plans to marry her off for her inheritance. "Well, as of right now, I've removed myself from the situation and there's no way on God's green earth he can find me."

She shook her head. She thought she couldn't run away, but even the alphabet agencies couldn't track her here.

"Running away isn't an option. If you leave your stallion, another will take you for his own. Stallions provide protection."

"From whom? Other stallions?" Bethany snorted. "That sounds like a good line, and it worked a long time for the Mob, but it's a load of horseshit." She shook her head again. "Seems like he's trying to convince you you have to do what he says so he can protect you from other males, but really it's just keeping you under his thumb."

Idrissa sipped her water, her expression thoughtful.

"I guess the point I'm trying to make is never stop standing up for what you want. They will try to intimidate you, but they only have power as long as you let them have it." Bethany eyed her companion critically. "You're big enough to take him on. I think if he tried to threaten or pressure you 'back to your place', if you stood up to him and assertively told him no, I think it'd make him change his tactics pretty quick."

Bethany lapsed into silence and wondered how much of her own advice she could implement with her father. Had she really been agreeing to his manipulations? Looking back over her life in Kentucky, the truth hit her square between the eyes. The phrase 'that's how it's done' ricocheted through her head and she clenched her jaw. *Time to change how it's done.*

"Well, shit."

"I beg your pardon?" Idrissa's head came up.

"I just realized I'm doing the same thing you are. Only it's with my father."

"Your father is the Stallion of the herd?"

"Something like that. Or he'd like to think so." Bethany snorted. "We call it Head of Household. He thinks he's the Man, the one in charge, and no one can say no to him." She clenched her fists, her nails biting into her palms. "I've been going right along with it." Her grin surprised them both. "Until now."

"Oh? Have you escaped his influence, Mare Bethany?" Idrissa cocked her head, her eyes curious.

"In more ways than one. I'm here. He can't find me, no matter the power or influence he wields." Her grin morphed into a smirk. "And until I'm missing long term, he can't use the money." The idea of sticking it to her father gave Bethany a warm and fuzzy feeling, but she sobered.

"I'll have to go back home, eventually." She brushed her fingers along the diaphanous curtains, the fine material sliding over her skin. "But maybe by then I'll have an idea how to take my inheritance and use it to finish my degree."

"I don't understand all your words, but I wish you luck in facing your paternal Stallion."

"Yeah, well, I'm probably gonna need it. But that doesn't help you right now." Bethany met Idrissa's blue gaze. "General Warrick wants you back in your place, whatever that means, but we have to make him see he'd much rather have you as a valued partner rather than a broodmare. We have to convince him you are more than just your gender." She gave Idrissa a half smile. "My boobs don't talk. Do yours?"

"What?" Idrissa looked perplexed.

"My breasts." Bethany pointed to her chest. "Mine don't talk, do yours?"

"Of course not. Why would you ask such a thing?"

"Because we have to make the males see that our value isn't in our bodies, but in the person inside. Warrick wants you in your place. We have to show him he's got the location wrong."

Idrissa grimaced. "And how will we do that?"

"Give him a new map. Your place is at his side, not in a gilded cage or corral." Bethany's smile faded. "It won't be easy. He has no reason, yet, to change. Let's see if we can give him one."

****

Morning wafted through the windows of Idrissa's barn and brought the sweet scents of rain and horse to Bethany's nose. She stretched and sat up, scanning the elegant room from her place on an especially large divan. *I supposed if I wore the latter half of a horse, I'd need something large to sit on.* Her stomach growled in protest and she wondered what centaurs ate. *Lordy, I hope they don't bend in half and graze.*

For all her horse-like body, Idrissa had been a great conversationalist. Despite her being locked away as Warrick's possession, she knew much of what occurred in the village and seemed to hold her stallion in high regard. They'd discussed ways Idrissa could siphon power from Warrick without being outright confrontational.

"It can be little tricky. The idea is to make him think it's all his choice and idea." Bethany had shrugged. "Is it manipulative? Hell yeah, but the direct approach doesn't seem to be working. The main goal is to find balance between you, and make you both happy."

Idrissa hadn't looked convinced. "I have never seen the general happy."

"Maybe this is exactly what he needs, then." Bethany had winked. "The other thing we should do is change the way we respond to him. He's used to telling you what to do and when to do it, and no one has ever given him any resistance. My nanny used to say children are master manipulators and they teach you how to parent."

"General Warrick is not a child."

"No, but the principle still applies. He won't change his behavior until you change yours, and how you respond." Bethany had winked. "It's time for him to go to school."

A side door Bethany hadn't noticed opened and another female centaur entered carrying a tray of food. Bethany didn't recognize most of it, but the scents of fruit, porridge, and bread filled the barn's main room.

"Thank you." Bethany nodded to the other woman and she jerked in surprise as if she hadn't expected the mythical beast to speak. Her hair and coat shone a lovely sorrel, but Bethany only got to see her backside when the centaur rushed back out the way she'd come.

Great. Now I'm the boogeyman.

Speaking of boogeymen, she'd arrived in a world filled with the myths from her home. *How the heck am I going to get back?* And the bigger question: Did she even want to go home?

She'd given Idrissa some great advice on dealing with the males, but had applied none of it in her own life. *Which makes me a hypocrite.* Dismay filled her gut as she stuffed a piece of sweet fruit in her mouth.

Bethany sat alone with her thoughts until Idrissa emerged from her bedroom, a closed-off stall decorated much like Bethany imagined Rapunzel's tower to look like. Ornate carvings and paints made the place cheery. *I guess you have to do something to convince yourself it's not really a prison.*

"Good morning." Bethany gestured at the tray. "Someone brought you breakfast, but I think I frightened her away."

Idrissa wore a blue half-tank that showed off her arms and the golden armbands wrapped around her biceps. A matching gold tiara sat on her head and gold bangles clung to each wrist and ankle. She looked every inch a queen of the centaurs.

"Wow, you look powerful." Bethany tried not to feel bad about her untucked plaid flannel shirt and jeans. *Talk about underdressed.*

"Thank you, Mare Bethany. I decided if I wanted more power I should dress like I deserved it." Idrissa gave her a rueful smile as she ate the bread from the tray.

"Smart. Sometimes it's all about presentation." There'd been hundreds of times she'd swum among the political sharks in her father's circles with nothing but her dress, her jewelry, and her wits to guard her. "People see what they want to see. You just have to give them the right vision."

Idrissa gazed at her with speculation. "Perhaps we can find you more appropriate attire as the guest of the Lead Mare."

Bethany snorted. "I'm a guest now, am I?"

Idrissa winked. "It's all about presentation, no?"

Bethany laughed. "Yes, it is."

Before either of them could say more, the doors to the barn opened and one of the burly guards stepped across the threshold, surveying the inside.

"Mare Bethany, you are summoned to General Warrick's quarters."

Anger surged in her chest, but she deliberately turned toward the guard and gave him a polite smile. "Thank you for the message. Let him know I'll be there as soon as I've finished my meal." She turned her shoulder to him, the equivalent of a horse presenting its tail to end a conversation, and smiled at Idrissa.

The guard stood flummoxed, his mouth agape in surprise. The tension rose with the silence, but Bethany stood firm.

"Have you a bath here, Lead Mare? I didn't see one when I arrived and it's been a long time since I've bathed."

Idrissa's mouth twitched as she fought a smile. The guard growled and took another step inside the barn. "You will come with me now, Mare Bethany."

"No, I won't. I will attend when I'm finished with my meal." Bethany didn't even turn her head.

"She has given her answer, Stal. Inform the general she'll be along as soon as she's eaten." Idrissa's voice held steel and she gestured him out with both hands.

The guard snorted like an affronted horse and backed awkwardly out the door as Idrissa herded him ahead of her. Then she closed the door and leaned her forehead against it, her shoulders shaking.

"Are you all right, Idrissa?" Bethany rose and stepped closer.

"Oh, sweet Epona!" She sounded breathless. "That was the best reaction I've seen in so long. He truly thought he could intimidate you." She shook her head, but her smile soon faded. "General Warrick will not be pleased."

"No, but he will have to make an effort either to be patient, or to come get me himself. And I'll still remind him that civility will get him a more favorable response than bullying."

"We will see if he manages to find his civility, Mare Bethany." Idrissa gave her a solemn stare. "It has been sorely lacking of late."

Bethany swallowed against her nervousness. "Then I'd best be prepared. Got any of that "appropriate attire" you were mentioning before?"

CHAPTER SIX

Mack woke with a start, his heart pounding and his breath silent. He listened hard, waiting for things to make sense. Nothing moved in the underbrush around him beyond the wind, but the air smelled of rain. He sat up, suppressing a groan. *I'm getting too old for this shit.*

He'd spent a good six hours waiting for Sergeant Bryant to find him, but he'd neither heard or seen anything remotely human in the woods, and the cavalry had moved off, taking their torches and mounts with them. Eventually, he'd found a hollow log in which to hole up, and caught some shut-eye, but it'd been fitful.

Mack stretched and scanned the forest around him, hoping to catch any sign of Bryant. He'd known this would be a clusterfuck from the beginning, but it had grown to world-class overnight. He just hoped Barnes would obey the orders and take the rest of the team home. The fewer men who ended up wherever he was, the better.

Mack rolled to his feet and inspected what gear had come with him. He still had his sidearm and his pack, but the lantern remained in his home world. Digging through the pack, he kept an eye on the world around him. It appeared to be a serene forest with birds twittering in the canopy above his head, but some of the sounds he'd heard during the night convinced him otherwise. He withdrew a bottle of water from his pack and took a swig, listening for the odd sounds now.

The wind rustled the trees and crickets called from the underbrush, but nothing else stirred in his vicinity. Mack capped his bottle and tucked it away, wondering how the hell he'd be able to track Ms. Stanton in this slightly odd forest. The trees themselves gave him the heebie-jeebies. His shoulder blades itched from the sensation of being watched. When he turned a full circle, casually inspecting the trees, nothing with sentience met his gaze. But the sensation remained.

Mack shouldered his pack and kept his motions relaxed as he flipped the safety on his Glock. Something told him he'd been wise not to start a fire. Nothing in the forest around him had changed, but the attention on him had sharpened. He checked his rough campsite for anything left behind while he surveyed the forest for motion in his peripheries.

His heartbeat thundered in his ears, but nothing out of the ordinary tripped his radar. *What the hell is watching me?* After checking the log thoroughly for his belongings, Mack followed the trail back to the place where he'd entered the forest. Whatever watched him kept pace and he gritted his teeth against the urge to call out.

Maybe it's Bryant.

But the sergeant would've made herself known, not skulk in the bushes. This was something else, and in all probability, something deadly. The hair on the back of Mack's neck stood up, but he forced himself to keep moving.

Instead of entering the open area covered in paving stones, Mack skirted around the outside, looking for the tracks he'd seen in the woods of Kentucky. The breeze ruffled the leaves over his head and filled the air with the scent of autumn. He paused beside a thick trunk with deeply ridged bark and searched the clearing before him.

Nothing moved beyond the branches over his head. Mack remained in his position for several more minutes, listening and watching for signs of company, but the trees withheld whatever secrets they carried. *At least the tingling in my damn nose has stopped.*

Mack's gaze dropped to the ground and he studied the many footprints stamped into the dusty trail. Unshod horse hooves of various size and shape led away from the site. *Good to know I didn't imagine the cavalry.* He'd been lucky to avoid their notice.

Mack studied the prints he could see for human boots, but only hoof crescents filled his gaze. Either Ms. Stanton hadn't come this way or the guys on horseback took her with them. *I'm betting on the latter.*

Listening hard, Mack inhaled and searched the woods for intruders. *Who am I kidding?* I'm *the intruder here.* At least, he assumed he'd arrived in a place different than Kentucky. With the disappearance of his team and his First Sergeant, all evidence pointed to having traveled somewhere.

Stop stalling.

Mack hated stepping into the open, but he'd seen no one and heard nothing constituting a threat. He eased his way onto the edge of the path, careful not to leave to many of his own footprints. The scrutiny from his unknown observer continued, but seemed less intense as he walked along the trail.

The prints showed the cavalry troop had moved at a slow pace and he almost looked away from the ground. But an odd shaped mark in the dirt arrested his motion. Mack crouched and picked up a leaf obscuring the print. A pointed toe and a separate heel sat clearly in the trail, missed by all the horses' hooves.

Mack raised his gaze to the trail ahead. *They made her*

walk? A few more bootprints showed up among the unshod crescents and he followed along, keeping his own off the dirt. The trees gave way to grasslands and some of the grass heads rose above his shoulders. The air smelled of grain ripening in the sun and grass as he skulked through the stalks. The wind rattled the fronds until it reached almost a screaming pitch.

Damn, I don't remember the wind being that fierce.

It took him a few heartbeats to realize it wasn't the wind making the sound. Mack jerked his gaze into the brilliant blue sky just in time to see a meteor heading straight for him.

Aw, shit, that's nice. What're the odds?

He tried to calculate where the meteor would hit and bolted perpendicular to it to escape. Oddly, the meteor seemed to follow him and he spun just as it crashed into the turf no more than thirty yards behind him. The impact threw him to the ground just as heat and flame shot over his head. Mack rolled to keep the flames from catching his clothes and scrambled to his feet to escape the brush fire.

He only had to run a few feet before the flames appeared to stop in a perfect circle around the impact. Mack paused and cautiously glanced over his shoulder. The meteor thrashed on the ground as if experiencing death throes.

What the hell?

Shrieking filled the air and a flailing mass churned in the center of the impact site. Flames licked in concentric circles around the thrashing creature, pulsing in time with flashes of light. A hum rose, the frequency growing louder and louder until another explosion rocked the grasslands.

Again, Mack was knocked off his feet as heat and light emblazoned the world. He threw his hands up over his eyes as debris rained down over him, bits of ash and grass smelling a lot like burnt feathers. He sat up and scanned the smoldering field, ducking when something grazed his head. He caught it and held up a brilliant orange feather that glinted gold when he turned it.

Little sparks seemed to trail behind it as he moved it through the air, but they didn't worry him half as much as the flames encroaching on his position in the grass. Mack scrambled up and tried to gauge which direction would get him out of the flames fastest. The ashes in the crater stirred as if the wind kicked them up, but the air around him lay still. He frowned and shifted closer, his curiosity overriding his preservation instinct.

What the hell is that?

Something pushed its way out of the soft gray flakes at the bottom of the impact crater. A head remarkably similar to a bird rose, followed by a long neck and bare shoulders. As he watched, the body sprouted what looked like feathers, similar in color to the one he held. The beak opened and a plaintive shriek rent the air. Mack slapped his hands to his ear as the creature extended its scaly arms and awkwardly flapped a few times, feathers growing like magic.

Magic.

He glanced at the feather in his fingers. It matched the plumage of the creature whistling and flapping on the ground. Sparks shot from the ends of its growing feathers and little flames licked along its crest and tail. The body enlarged as it flapped its wings harder and it met Mack's gaze with a glowing red eye.

Aw, shit.

The thing lurched to its taloned feet and shook itself, new tendrils of flame skating off the ends of its limbs. Mack swallowed hard and took off running out away from the forest. Something told him he'd be safest if he found water—a stream or a pond—anything to keep him from burning alive. Grass fires were nothing to sneeze at and he'd be damned before he died in one caused by a freak meteor. A freak meteor giving chase, no less.

He clutched the feather tight in his fist as he pounded

through the grass, searching the ground for signs of a waterway. Where the hell were the cottonwoods or junipers? The landscape rose in front of him then dipped sharply and he ducked into a roll as something hot and screeching shot overhead. Mack tumbled to a halt with a splash, waist deep in a chuckling stream.

He lay flat as the flaming creature strafed over him again, its voice adding to the cacophony of the blood pounding in his ears. *Holy shit, is that thing a phoenix?* The bird circled around in the smoky sky, its attention pinned on him before eventually losing interest. Mack slumped in the water and tried to make sense of everything.

Where the fuck had he ended up?

****

Bethany crossed her arms over her chest and faced the general with her patented stoic expression in place as he ranted. She'd been subjected to his fury for at least twenty minutes and found it harder and harder to keep her cool. From laughter. He blustered and snorted just like an angry horse, and while she knew he could kill her, his violence remained relatively controlled.

Maybe it's the clothing Idrissa gave me.

"You will come when I call because I'm the general!" His shout made her jump as he rounded on her, his eye blazing.

"General, while I'm your guest, you have much control, but I'm not your servant." Bethany tried to keep her voice even.

"You're female. Females are meant to serve."

She blinked back some of her rising anger and tried to think of his issues as part of the problem he wanted her to solve. Taking a deep breath, she raised her chin and gave him a tight smile.

"And that is the root of your problem."

"I beg your pardon?" His own head came up and his nostrils flared.

"You should in this instance, but that's not what I'm asking for. I want you to get some perspective." Taking a deep breath, she uncrossed her arms and tried to relax. "You told me you wanted me to find out why your Lead Mare is unhappy and tell you what you could do to fix the problem. Isn't that what you said?"

General Warrick stopped pacing and leaned forward with his hands flat on his desk. "I asked *you* to fix it."

Bethany shrugged with her hands out in helplessness. "I can't. I'm not the source of the irritation. I can give you pointers on what you need to do from Lead Mare Idrissa's perspective, but I can't fix the problem myself."

Warrick scowled. "Are you saying I'm the source of the problem?"

Aren't men almost always the source? Okay, that wasn't fair, but most of the issues Bethany faced in her life had either been started or perpetuated by men.

"Idrissa sees it that way. You're going to have to convince her you're making changes." When he opened his mouth to say something, Bethany held up her hand to stop him. "She's pretty smart, General. She'll know if you're playing a game. She wouldn't be Lead Mare if she didn't."

"I'm aware of her intelligence." If he'd had tall ears he would've flattened them.

Really? Because you're acting like she's a mindless pet.

Bethany beat her irritation back behind her eyes. "Do you want to hear my suggestions and analysis, or do you want things to remain the same, General? The choice is yours this time."

His expression settled into cold patience and he nodded. "Very well, Mare Bethany. What do you suggest?"

There's hope for you yet, big guy. "Treat her like a person you respect and like."

Warrick snorted. "I do treat her like a person."

"No, you treat her like a female."

"She *is* a female."

"See, that's where you're missing the point." Bethany gestured to her own body. "The shape of her body is irrelevant to how you treat her. You must see beyond the breasts and lady parts to the person inside. You need to start treating her like you would your own men or an equal male in your circles." She paused, wondering if he could hear the rest without having a hissy fit. *Won't know until you put it out there.* "Right now, you treat your Lead Mare and all your subsidiary mares like chattel or possessions. They aren't either of those things, they're people. This is why Idrissa is rejecting you. You've already relegated her to nothing more than an object to show your prestige. She's not a possession, General. She's a partner and a confidant."

"Of course she's my confidant." He shook his head. "This has always been the way."

"Have you shown her in your actions?" Bethany pointed back toward the barn where Idrissa stayed. "This morning you sent someone, *sent*, to summon me, as if I'm some sort of dog at your beck and call. You couldn't be bothered to come yourself. Do you do that to Idrissa, too?"

"Of course. I'm busy." He gestured to the village. "I'm in charge here and my time is limited."

"No one is criticizing your use of your time, General. But if you leave the interactions you have with your Lead Mare, who is essentially your wife, to an underling, you will lose all of her respect. And you'll lose her."

"This doesn't fix the problem." His scowl deepened.

"No, but it does make you aware of some of the things that can be fixed." Bethany took a deep breath to find her patience. "Let me ask you another question. Do you love the Lead Mare?"

"What?"

Bethany held up her hands in a placating gesture. "You don't have to answer. I know that's a personal question.

But just consider the answer. Love is an emotion based on respect and admiration. You need to figure out how you feel about Idrissa and that will help you repair the relationship you have."

"I don't understand all this emotional female...stuff." He waved one hand with a frown.

"It's not just female stuff, General." Bethany courted her patience with the reminder that he was at least talking about it. "All sentient beings have emotions, male or female. The trick here is for you to get beyond the fear of them."

"Fear? I'm not afraid of anything." He raised his chin and shot her a baleful look.

Yeah, right. Tell me another one.

"Very well, General. You wanted my efforts on your behalf, and this is what I've given you. The problem here doesn't just lie with your Lead Mare. To get back her affections, you're going to have to make some adjustments to your campaign."

He narrowed his eyes. "What campaign?"

"The one to win back the heart of your Lead Mare and those of your harem. Let me know when you have a plan of action, and I'll bring your terms back to Idrissa." Bethany bowed. "Good day, general."

"This is impossible, Mare Bethany."

"No more impossible than flying to the moon. But it's been done."

General Warrick snorted. "Do you fly?"

"What?"

"Do you fly?"

"Honey, if I could fly, I wouldn't still be here in your village. Why?"

"Because it's more likely that I sprout wings and soar around the moon than it is I'll ever understand female emotions."

Bethany scowled. "Better learn they're not just for females. That'll be a huge improvement." She smoothed her expression. "Look, what I'm trying to tell you is the ladies aren't enjoying how you treat them and you're not likely to change that until you understand their perspective. They're...centaurs, not merely females, and until you see them that way, they aren't likely to change their treatment of you."

"What are you suggesting?" Warrick didn't look convinced, but Bethany had said her piece.

"I'm not suggesting anything. I'm telling you if you want Idrissa and the others to wish to be with you, you'll have to change how you look at and interact with them." Bethany shrugged. "We have a saying back home. You get what you give. What have you been giving? Think about that. I'll be with the Lead Mare should you have need of me, General."

She inclined her head and retreated toward the doors of his office, wondering where she got the gumption to tell a centaur general how to treat women. *And why haven't I ever told my father the same?*

CHAPTER SEVEN

Bethany dressed in her flannel shirt and jeans before setting out at a walk beyond the edges of the village. The day had started out warm and clear, but thick clouds built on the horizon to the west and the humidity filled the air. She didn't have a destination in mind, but her feet took her in the direction of the forest. The lands of the dryads. *What the heck is a dryad anyway?*

A few days earlier, the centaurs had battled a brush fire sweeping across their plains and Warrick said it had been caused by a phoenix at the end of its life cycle. She'd tried to take him at his word, but it sounded like something a primitive people would use to explain the unexplainable. Instead of lightning causing a fire, they created a phoenix. The damage had been small and no one sustained injuries. The general said they'd searched the impact site for feathers, but none had been found.

No doubt because the source was lightning.

When she'd asked about the feathers, he told her phoenix feathers brought the bearer increased health and granted protection from magical attack. She could see why the centaurs would want such a prize, but searching for phoenix feathers at the site of a lightning strike seemed a fool's errand. She'd kept her thoughts to herself, and as she crossed the edge of the burn scar, Bethany shook her head in amusement.

The terrain around her shifted from grasslands to retreating forest and the scents of pines and leaf debris perfumed the air. Bethany found a fallen log and sat down on its smooth surface, letting some of the tension drain from her body. She ran her hands over her face. What was she going to do about the centaurs? She'd been the liaison between General Warrick and his mares for the last three weeks, and no one seemed willing to compromise. While the men were overbearing and arrogant, the women had been hurt enough to keep a tight rein on whatever power they could glean, and refused to bend.

Ironically, she'd made friends with Warrick, their meetings often turning into intellectual discussions about male versus female reactions, and similarities between their species. When he wasn't telling her the foibles of females, Warrick had a sharp wit and a well developed sense of humor. He could be quite charming if he put his mind to it. Unfortunately, he had little patience for the demands of change from his mares.

"Ugh, how am I going to get them to bend?" She braced her elbows on her knees. "And how the hell am I going to get home?" She examined the dried grass beneath her boots.

According to the centaurs, the doorway between words only opened on ceremonial days. So far she hadn't been able to figure out when those occurred. When she'd asked, the answers resembled riddles—when day and night court, when the shadows swallow the sun, when the sun eats the night, when Epona's moon shines. The next wasn't due to occur for a few months and the centaurs didn't know if the doorways would even open.

Getting home seems less than likely.

But did she even want to go home?

What she'd told Idrissa about her father was true and she'd never get to use it if she didn't go home. But if she didn't go home, she wouldn't have to. *That's a cop-out.* She couldn't argue, but in practical terms she was stuck with the centaurs and their domestic gender issues. She had no idea how she'd sort them out. Hell, she couldn't sort out her own species. Bethany groaned and covered her face with her hands.

The lilting notes of a flute pulled Bethany's head up and she scanned the world around her. Something moved from the trees behind her and her jaw dropped as she stared, abashed. A satyr, a real benighted satyr skipped into the clearing before her, playing a reed pipe. Great curling horns of a Dall's sheep sprouted from his head and a thick pelt of dark hair covered his legs as he danced. The music wove a haunting melody around her and some of her concerns faded into the background.

"Why so sad, dear lady?" He paused before her and offered her a coaxing smile. "Perhaps I can play your sorrows away."

Bethany wondered if she'd been worrying too much. What were her problems, anyway? She couldn't quite remember and the music in the satyr's voice lulled away her stress. A thick, warm balm flooded over her and she sighed with relief. His smile broadened.

"Come with me. I shall grant you all that you desire."

What did she desire, again? Peace, pleasure, and relaxation. She found herself nodding and leaned toward him, reaching for the hand he offered. The smile darkened with sensual promise.

Before she could touch his fingers, a loud report broke the silence and the satyr jerked his hand back with a snarl. Blood dripped from a ragged wound in his palm and his face warped into a nasty sneer with sharp teeth protruding through his lips. Bethany gasped and scrambled backwards behind the log, panic surging through her. The satyr bolted away into the trees with a bleating complaint.

Dear God, that sounded like a gun shot.

Bethany shook her head, trying to clear the fog drenching her thoughts. She searched the woods around her, her heart thudding in her throat. A voice told her she should run back toward the centaur camp, but given the satyr, running blind anywhere seemed just as stupid as sitting still. At least she'd see what came at her in the clearing.

Bethany waited and listened hard, letting her eyes unfocus to catch any movement from the forest. Nothing came to her senses. The satyr's passage had faded into the distance and only the wind through the trees broke the tense silence.

Then the shrubs to her left stood up.

Bethany yelped and lurched to her feet, backing away from the odd creature. Bipedal and binocular, it towered over her by a good eight inches and wore all black. She scanned the body cataloging all the items she recognized.

Combat boots laced up to the shins. Black canvas cargo pants with millions of pockets. Batman-like utility belt with odd implements, including a gun holster complete with protruding pistol butt. A black vest resembling Kevlar covered the broad chest and black and brown face paint obscured the skin around piercing blue eyes the color of a Kentucky summer sky.

Those eyes took in her appearance with the same frank appraisal she'd offered then scanned the forest behind her. She swore the creature looked human, male, and from her own world as he stepped closer.

"Bethany Stanton?"

Bethany blinked. *That sounds like American English.*

"Yes?"

"I'm Major Stephen McMacken, US Army. I'm here to take you home."

"What?"

The eyes snapped to her face. "Major Stephen McMacken, US Army."

"Yeah, I got that part. What are you doing here?"

Frustration tightened the lips in the blackened face. "I'm here to rescue you."

Bethany gaped. "Where did you come from? How did you get here?"

"We came from Kentucky. Your father sent us."

"Us?"

"Do you think we could leave the twenty questions until after we get out of here?" The eyes flicked toward the trees again as a low rumble hit their ears. No doubt the centaurs had heard the gun shot clearly in the still morning air. While they weren't close, sound carried easily across the grasslands and they'd soon have centaurian company.

Bethany stared at the tense man and tried to make up her mind. He said he'd come to take her home, but he'd also said her father had sent him. *Guess it's time to make my decision, like it or not.* But she hesitated. How the hell had Major McMacken gotten here? Was the doorway between the worlds still open?

"Wait, how did you get here, exactly, Major? Is the rift still open?"

"I came through the archaeological site two nights ago." He took a step toward her. "As far as I know it's still open. So let's get going before it closes, shall we?"

"That's impossible. I have it on good authority it closed. Three weeks ago."

"Don't know what to tell you other than I came through two days ago and it's time we get back home. So let's go."

Bethany sat on the log and crossed her arms over her chest. "I think you should relax a little. You said my father sent you?"

"Let's go, Ms. Stanton. I'll explain on the way." The major reached for her, but she scooted out of reach.

"No."

"What?" The blue gaze zeroed in on her.

"No, I'm not going back with you. Tell my father you didn't find me or you found pieces of my body, I don't really care. But at the moment, I'm not going back to Kentucky. And most likely, neither are you."

"Dammit, Ms. Stanton, I don't have time for this."

Bethany snorted. "Honey, I suspect you have more time than you know. Looks like you're stuck here like I am."

He growled. "My mission is to bring you home and I will. Stop being a spoiled little rich girl and let's go."

"Is that what you think? Is that what they told you, that I'm spoiled and running away?" Bethany laughed in disbelief. "Damn, Daddy must really need that money for the campaign." She rose and took a few steps along the trail toward the centaur village. "I'm not spoiled, Major. I'm just looking for my independence."

"This is a helluva way to do it." He advanced on her, his face implacable as his menace. "I don't care why you came here, Ms. Stanton. It's my job to get you home to where you belong."

"I don't belong there any more than I belong here. But at least here I have choices."

"Not today."

She whooped in surprise as he caught her around the legs and hauled her over his shoulder in a fireman's carry. Then he turned and sprinted—*sprinted*—away from the increasing sounds of hooves against the ground. Bethany wanted to scream with frustration, but she bounced against his shoulder too hard to catch her breath and call out.

"What...are you...doing? Let...me...go." She had no force in her voice, but she squirmed against his hold. "The...rift is...closed."

"Hold still, dammit." He tightened his arms around her legs and hips, and kept running. "I'm taking you home."

"I'd rather you...take me...to prison."

"That can be arranged."

They crashed through the trees, errant limbs swatting her ass as they passed. Fury welled in her gut and she slowly built up the breath the scream, despite the jolts of his shoulder against her belly. When he paused to make a directional decision, Bethany shrieked as loud and hard as should could, praying the centaurs would hear her.

"God dammit, shut up." The Major snarled as he lurched into another run toward the stream she'd seen as the centaurs escorted her from the trees.

Oh, shit. Not the lamps.

"No. You have to stop." She struggled harder. He couldn't enter the woods near the stream. He'd be turned into a lamp, or worse. They'd both suffer for defiling the sacred grove. "You can't go in there. Stop!"

"Stop struggling."

"No. You don't understand. *I don't want to be a lamp.*" Bethany slammed her fist into his kidneys from the back.

"What the fuck!" He released her as he went down, rolling away to keep from crushing her.

Bethany hit the ground and scrambled to her feet, desperate to get back to the grasslands. *I won't be a lamp. I won't be a lamp, I won't be a lamp.* She bolted from the sounds of tinkling water and the lurid glow of the transformed princess. She heard a vicious curse behind her, but didn't pause. The open land beyond the trees beckoned and she pushed her body harder.

All her breath *whooshed* out of her as she slammed to the ground in a flying tackle from behind. She yelped in outrage and pain, but the man had a tight grip as he rolled her onto his chest.

"Stop, Ms. Stanton. I'm not trying to hurt you."

"Then let me go." She kicked at him, struggling to break free.

"I can't do that." He grunted and gritted his teeth, his eyes blazing. "Calm down. I have to get you home."

"Home isn't in that direction. You're going the wrong

way. I don't want to be a lamp."

"What the hell are you going on about?"

"Didn't you see the lamp by the stream?" Bethany struggled harder, but his arms tightened.

"No. I was too busy trying to catch your ass."

Bethany sighed and relaxed against his hard body. She tried not inhale the spicy scent of his sweat, but it filled her nose and sent inappropriate reactions throughout her body. "I'm sorry, Major. But you were going the wrong way. The lamp was a princess."

"What?" McMacken raised his eyebrows.

Bethany shrugged helplessly. "A princess. Don't you know the story of the twelve dancing princesses?"

"No." His brows lowered over his brilliant blue eyes.

"Just take my word for it." Bethany shoved against his chest, but he held her fast. "The Twelve Dancing Princesses were turned into lamps for doing something wrong in the dryads' sacred grove and now serve as a warning to others all over the forest."

"Are you serious?"

She nodded and his grip loosened just before he rolled her to the ground. She thought about running from him again, but decided it wasn't worth the effort. When he stood over her, he offered her a hand up. She looked at the hand then raised her gaze to those lovely blue eyes. His lips tightened in exasperation and his shook his hand with an imperative motion.

"Let's go, Ms. Stanton."

"I don't want to go back to Kentucky, Major." She sat up, draping her arms over her knees. "I might not have expected to come here, but now that I have, I choose not to go back to my father's estate."

"It's my mission to get you home safe and sound, Ms. Stanton."

Bethany ignored his hand and got up on her own. "If you take me back to Kentucky, I'll be neither of those things."

"I highly doubt that. Your father and fiancé want to see you."

White-hot anger surged through her. "I just bet they do." Bastards still tried to control her life, even from the other side of the rift. "No. I'm not going with you."

"Dammit, Ms. Stanton—"

"Go home if you can, Major. Tell them you didn't find me. Hell, tell them you only found my body if it helps your sense of honor. But I'm not going back with you. I'd rather take my chances with the centaurs."

"Enough with the stories, Ms. Stanton. I'm sure you can make up some great ones, but we need to get back to our world." The major reached for her again, but froze as the sounds of the drumming hooves had steadily increased.

Bethany backed away from him, her jaw clenched. "I'm not making the centaurs up, Major."

Before he could reply, Warrick and his cohort of men burst upon them, shouting war cries and brandishing their pikes. Surprise hit the Major's face just before his expression hardened into impassivity. She had to admire his poise as he scanned the horse-men circling them. She could see him calculating his chances of getting away. *Translation—not bloody likely.* And thank goodness. She'd rather kiss a whole troupe of overbearing centaur males than return to Senator Stanton and his sycophantic protégé, John Coolidge.

"Friends of yours?"

"More like allies." Bethany bit her lip. Most military men she knew didn't stand for capture very well. "Just don't make any sudden moves, okay? They're faster than they look and they're a helluva lot heavier."

"And you'd rather stay here?" McMacken held his hands up in the universal sign of surrender and eyed Warrick as the general skidded to a halt in front of him.

A grim scowl twisted the centaur's face. "By the gods,

there are more of you?" Warrick jabbed a finger in Bethany's direction. "Did you call more to come for you?"

"What? No." She crossed her arms over her chest. "This guy just showed up out of nowhere." She glared at the Major. "And I told him to go back home without me."

"I can't do that."

"No, you *won't* do that. This is a choice issue for you."

"Bind him." Warrick's voice held exasperation.

The Major tensed and she prayed he wouldn't go for his weapon. The last thing she needed was the Elder Council convinced she'd brought a deadly weapon along with her mythological presence into their world. She stared at McMacken, trying to catch his eyes, but he only watched those taking him into custody. *Please, please, don't do anything stupid.*

McMacken remained docile, but she didn't think he'd stay that way for long given the expression on his face. She clenched her jaw and turned to talk to Warrick, but he staunchly ignored her and she was shoved together with the major as the centaurs marched them back toward the camp. Crushed grass mixed with the heady scents of leather and man, much different from the musky horse scent from their escorts. McMacken said nothing, but frustration settled in tense lines across his shoulders.

Bethany sighed. This day just got better and better. And she'd gotten nowhere in her plans to help Idrissa or Warrick. Now she had another problem with the major.

"Did my father really send you to come get me?"

"Yes." He stared straight ahead.

"Why?"

"What do you mean, 'why'? You ran away."

"I didn't run away. I ended up here. Do you really think I haven't tried to get home?"

"I don't know, Ms. Stanton. You seemed pretty set on staying."

Bethany exhaled some of her own frustration. She

couldn't argue with that. "How long have you been here, again?"

"Three days."

"Three days. I've been here *three weeks*. I've been trying to figure out how to get home that whole time, but the centaurs aren't very trusting. It's not like I could wander out to the ceremonial site to check if the rift stayed open. Today was the first day I got to go out on my own. So thanks for screwing that up."

"I didn't screw *anything* up, sweetheart. You were the one who sabotaged our escape attempt. If you hadn't struggled, we could've been well on our way back."

"Oh yeah? How are you going to 'get back' to our world, genius? Just shoot a hole through the dimensions with your pistol? Do you even know anything about this kind of world travel?"

"How do you know we aren't on some eccentric billionaire's movie set?" He glared back at her. "These could be elaborate costumes."

"Three weeks." She bared her teeth at him. "I've been here, with these people, for three weeks. I think I can tell between costumes and real. And let me tell you, these folks aren't fooling around." Then she laughed. "Just wait until you see the females. *Then* tell me they're fake."

"The breasts?"

"The centaurs." Bethany rolled her eyes.

"Why didn't you come back with me?" He sounded genuinely interested, but she didn't buy it for a second.

"It's, uh…personal."

"Against me specifically or something else?"

"Wow, aren't you arrogant?" Bethany shook her head. "Have you met my father, Major?"

"Yes." He didn't sound thrilled.

That's something at least.

"What about the man you call my fiancé? Met him yet?"

"Yes."

"Let me put it to you clearly so there's no doubt. I'd rather have a hard-core sex romp worthy of the tabloids with three of our centaur guards than return to either of the men you've met. M'kay?"

She gave him her perfected plastic smile as the escorts chuckled with amusement. The centaurs had been on the receiving end to her stubbornness for the last three weeks and probably enjoyed the reprieve.

Damn right they should be relieved. If she was stuck in this world with these folks, they'd better learn to treat a woman right because she was done being someone's submissive little girl, always looking pretty and perfect. She'd make her own decisions from now on.

The centaurs led them back to the camp and past Warrick's quarters. Unease slid through her as they neared the stockade. It looked like something out of a Revolutionary War-aged fort with sturdy poles sharpened to points. Inside they'd constructed an overhang which provided a crude stable for prisoners. Mud and straw made up the floor of the stockade, with nothing to sit on.

One of the guards crowded Major McMacken against the wall and lifted his bound hands toward the ceiling of the small overhang, binding them to a rafter. He reached for the Major's weapons, but Bethany slid between them before Mack could do anything.

"I'll get his equipment."

"Mare Bethany, you do not understand—"

"*I* don't understand?" Bethany stood her ground, lifting her chin. "He's from my world, of my people, and you're telling me I don't understand? Back down before you hurt yourself, stal, and let me disarm him."

The big guard glared down his nose at her, his human arms and chest flexing as he tried to intimidate her into submission. She'd played this game hundreds of times with the horses on her father's farm. Bigger didn't mean in control.

"Back off, stal. Now." She stepped forward, crowding him. The big guard hesitated, then took a few stiff steps back. "Good. Wait at the gate. I'll bring his things when I finish speaking to him."

He snorted, but retreated, and Bethany nodded to herself. *Damn right you step back.* She returned her attention to the man waiting with a stoic mask and thanked her lucky stars his hands remained bound. He struck her as a predator biding its time and something told her she might not want to be alone with him.

"What do you think you're doing?" His growl wouldn't carry more than the space between them as she reached for his belt.

"I'm making sure weapons from our world don't end up replicated over here. They don't have projectile weapons beyond bows and I'd like it to stay that way." She unbuckled the belt and tried to ignore the heat of his body in the leather. Touching the major like this seemed intimate and her neck prickled from the intensity of his gaze on her.

When she slid the belt out of the loops, her hands shook. She'd never touched a man with such familiarity unless alone in a bedroom with him. The absurdity of pulling off his belt in a stockade with several male centaurs watching warily made her face heat. Major McMacken smelled so damn good and she wished she could take his rescue, settle back, and let someone else make the decisions.

But she'd been doing that for far too long. *And that's what Daddy and John are hoping I'll do.*

"I'm sorry. Better they're with me than with them."

She slung the belt over her shoulder, the pistol butt thumping her in the breast. He chuckled when she grimaced.

"You know how to use one of those?"

She gave Mack an acidic look and pulled the pistol free before checking to make sure the safety was on. Against her father's wishes, she'd learned how to shoot with help of her brother Kevin. Though not an expert marksman like him, she could hit a moving target with both a rifle and a handgun.

"Want me to demonstrate on you?" She shoved the pistol back into the holster and fingered the rest of the equipment on the belt. "Kinda under-equipped for a rescue mission, aren't you?"

"We took only what we could carry that didn't require batteries." At her raised eyebrows, he added, "Didn't you notice your cell phone not working?"

Bethany blinked and slapped her pockets then laughed. "I didn't bring it with me. I didn't want the bastards to find me on my ride so I left it at home." She shrugged. "I haven't missed it."

"A senator's daughter doesn't miss her electronic leash?" McMacken shook his head. "Not buying it."

She shrugged again as she slid the gun holster off the belt. "I don't really care what you believe, Major. The reality is I don't have the phone and we're both stuck here." She gave him her plastic smile again. "I'll try to get you released soon."

Bethany swung away, tucking the weapon in her waistband under her shirt, and stomped over to the centaur guard. "I've disarmed him and he should be fine. I'd like to talk to General Warrick."

"I'm sorry, Mare Bethany. You are to stay here with the prisoner."

"What? Under whose orders?" Her hands tightened on the equipment belt.

"General Warrick's."

Bethany stared at the guard, astounded. "For what charge?"

"For endangering the centaurs by further incursion of humans." He reached for the belt in her hands and she stepped back. "Give me the belt, Mare Bethany."

Bethany snorted, raised her chin, and backed up more.

"If I'm just another prisoner, then he can keep his things. You have no right to them. Go back and tell your general if he chooses to treat me in this manner, he can expect me to respond in kind. You are dismissed, stal."

She turned sideways and looked down out of the corner of her eye, effectively dismissing him without turning her back. The guard bounced a little on his forelegs in a threat display, but she stood her ground until he whirled in a huff and slammed the stockade gate. Bethany dropped her shoulders and shook her head.

Frustration, indignation, and despair flashed through her before resignation came to roost. So much for her friendship with Warrick. *Back to the drawing board with regard to his trust.* She wanted to shout and scream at McMacken for ruining her carefully constructed rapport with the centaur general, but she suspected the major constituted only a small irritation. The female centaurs hadn't come around even with her liaising, and Warrick wasn't very patient.

Bethany sighed as she trudged to McMacken and tried think of something to say.

"Not so high and mighty anymore, huh, sweetheart?"

Bethany clenched her jaw as her temper flared. "You know, you could just say thank you for saving your stuff." She slammed his belt into his chest and let it fall. "Get your own bad self out of that, soldier boy."

"My weapon?"

"You won't need it."

Then she walked away from him before she burst into tears from frustration. Dear God, why was she surrounded by assholes, no matter the species? She almost stepped out from under the overhang when the sky opened up and rain poured from the sky in a deluge. *Great.* She backed against the wall and slid to the straw, dropping her head to her knees.

Just great.

CHAPTER EIGHT

Mack mentally kicked himself. There was no reason to take his frustration out on Ms. Stanton, especially when it appeared her status as favored had changed. Despite his preferences, they were stuck here and picking on her wouldn't change the situation. When she hunkered down out of the rain he swore under his breath. She wore nothing, but a brown and white plaid flannel shirt and jeans. She'd be soaked in moments.

"I'm sorry, Ms. Stanton. Do you think you could do me the favor of untying my hands?"

"You're the badass soldier. I'm sure your superpowers allow you to leap tall buildings in a single bound or magically untie ropes. Don't let me tarnish your reputation."

He clenched his jaw and tried to throttle his temper. They'd never get out of here dwelling on petty things like emotions.

"I admit normally my skills exceed belief, but even I usually have a team behind me. Think you could give me a hand here?"

A long suffering sigh accompanied another droop in her shoulders. She mumbled something like 'arrogant jerk' and 'manners', but unfolded herself from her crouch and returned to his side. She stood up on her toes, reaching for his hands to pull the knots securing them to the rafters of their enclosure. Her breasts pressed against his side, offering a far more welcome warmth. Mack tried to keep his mind on the mission, not on the softness of her body or the scent of her hair.

The tip of her tongue emerged from her pink lips as she concentrated and he had the oddest urge to kiss it.

What the fuck is wrong with me? He focused on the loosening ties at his wrists to keep his cock from rising at precisely the wrong moment. Each jostling movement of her body reminded his of what he'd been missing for weeks while on mission after mission. *Focus.*

At the last moment, Bethany lost her balance as she freed his hands and toppled into him with a gasp. He jerked his arms down just in time to catch her and steady her against his chest. She met his gaze and he fell into her rich hazel eyes.

He cleared his throat. "Are you okay?"

"Yes, fine, thank you." Bethany stepped back, tugging down the hem of her shirt in an effort to reclaim her composure. "You're hands are free so you should be set."

Mack nodded and rubbed his wrists where the twine had chaffed. "Can I get my weapon back, now, Ms. Stanton?"

She tilted her head to eye him with suspicion. He did his best to show innocence, but she snorted and grimaced at his attempt.

"Give me a good reason to hand it to you, Major. What's to keep you from going all out like a blaze of glory?"

He grunted his amusement. "Honestly? You."

She shook her head. "How would I stop you?"

"I'm supposed to bring you home safe and sound, not dead. More than likely you'd get yourself killed on my way out."

"I'd get myself killed?" She raised her chin and shook

her head. "Why? Because I'm a woman?"

Mack snorted. "No, because you're not a trained soldier."

"And *you* have no experience with centaurs, Major. You might have specialized military training, but you have no idea what to do about a completely different species without someone dying." She crossed her arms over her chest. "This isn't a quick smash-and-grab sort of thing we're stuck in. These are people and aware, and probably as good at being soldiers as you are, so more than likely, I'm the one keeping you alive."

Mack didn't believe her, but antagonizing Bethany further wouldn't get his pistol back. "That might be, but having my weapon would help me believe it. May I please have my Glock?"

"Wow, you do have manners when you want to use them." She reached behind her, tightening the wet shirt against her breasts and his cock took an interest, flexing beneath his fly. Mack gritted his teeth and tried to keep his expression bland as she handed over his weapon and belt. "Just keep the gun out of sight as much as possible. I'd just as soon they never develop firearms."

"The centaurs."

"Yes. And everyone else here."

"Where is here?" He buckled his equipment belt around his hips and scanned the stockade. The lodgepole fence rose too high to see much of anything beyond, but he'd shot a honest-to-God satyr trying to seduce her earlier. *Not to mention the phoenix.*

"From what I can tell it's an...alternate world filled with all the myths from our world." She grimaced, wrapping her arms around her waist to keep warm. "Hey look, I didn't say it makes a lot of sense, but when I came here, they told me humans were a myth. A kind of boogeyman to frighten their children at bedtime."

Bethany shivered and huddled against the stockade wall.

The sudden urge to wrap himself around her soft, yielding body grabbed Mack by the balls. Not that he'd noticed it was soft, lush, or even sweet scented. *Yeah, right. Nice try, jackass.*

But he couldn't stand to see her cold.

"Here, come over next to me out of the rain and we'll stay warmer together." Mack crouched against the wall in the center of the overhang and extended his arm.

Bethany raised her eyebrows and didn't move.

"Come on. There's no point in getting sick if we're both stuck here anyway. I don't bite." He waved his hand and Bethany snorted. "You said it yourself. I tend to shoot things."

"Heh."

But she pushed up and scuttled to his side, hunkering down again. He lifted his arm and settled it around her shoulders, flinching as the water seeped through his clothes. She exhaled a relieved sigh and snuggled closer.

"Damn, woman, you're soaked."

"My name is Bethany, and yes, I am. But you're warm and dry, so thank you, Major, for the heat." She laid her head against his chest and an odd sort of satisfaction bloomed inside him. When her arm wrapped across his belly, he resolutely ignored his cock's rejoicing.

"Very well, Bethany. You're welcome." Mack gently tightened his grip on her. "Do you really think this is an alternate world?"

"You got a better explanation for centaurs, dryads, and such? Who think *we're* the myths?"

Mack chuckled. "No, not yet, at least."

Bethany grunted with disdain. "Yeah, well, since you've been here all of three days, you haven't had enough time to do some fact-checking." She shivered again and he pulled her closer. "They don't have cell phones or anything electronic here. They don't have anything with wheels unless it's a cart, and most of the weaponry consists of spears, knives, bows, and their own limbs. Have you ever seen centaur hand-to-hand combat? It's unnerving."

"How so?" Mack didn't really care, but he liked listening to her voice. He'd never thought he'd be lonely, but being without his team for almost three days had triggered a desolation he'd never experienced before.

"You've done hand-to-hand, right?" He nodded and she snorted. "You have to keep track of only four limbs. When these guys go at it, they have six limbs, and four of those limbs have hard hooves at the ends of them." She shuddered. "It's the creepiest thing to see two guys grappling while their forelegs hold their opponent down. I understand warhorses, but this was too weird."

"Did you study warhorses because your dad owns a stable?"

"No, actually, I wrote a paper on the political influence of the military, and I focused on the great cavalries of the world. The Russian Cossacks, the Huns, even the Polish cavalries were some of the most influential groups and caused major turning points in several wars." Bethany yawned and rubbed her cheek on him. "Did you know the Army still has a 'cavalry'? They just don't use horses anymore." She snorted softly. "Seems silly to use the name without the animal."

"I don't know," Mack mused. "I think the phrase 'call in the cavalry' sounds better than saying 'call in those mobile guys with guns.'"

A rough shudder ran through Bethany's frame and he realized she was laughing. "Yeah, I have to agree with you there." She sighed again. "Why is it men are so much warmer than women, even in the cold?"

"Gigantothermy?"

Bethany pulled back. "What?"

He chuckled at her wide-eyed expression. "Gigantothermy. You know, men are larger with more muscle mass, which creates extra heat." He raised a teasing eyebrow. "Never heard the term?"

She blinked. "I know the term. I just never expected to hear it from a career military man."

The admiration in her voice set off an explosion of delight inside him. "The military actually recruited me after I graduated from UC Berkeley with my bachelor's in geologic sciences."

"Wait." Bethany laid her hand against his chest in mock amazement. "You're educated?"

He tried to ignore the pleasure radiating from her touch. "Yeah. Kinda. I can add..."

She grimaced. "Sorry. That sounded really snobbish."

"Maybe a little."

"So if you graduated in geology, why did you suddenly join military?"

"I looked really good in the fatigues. All the gay guys told me so." Mack winked and tilted his head with a coquettish smile.

She laughed as he'd hoped she would and nodded slowly. "Oh, I see. So you're part of the 'don't ask, don't tell' crew?"

"Well, now that you ask..." Where was all this coming from? He should be worrying about returning to his team and getting them home. But instead he flirted with the senator's daughter, and enjoyed every moment of it.

"No, really. Why did they recruit you when you were going for your degree?"

"At first, it was a good way to pay off the student loans without depending on mom and dad. I was a good athlete, but I wasn't all that interested in playing organized sports to get the scholarships ."

"You don't play well with others?" Bethany gave him a dry look.

"That's my line." He grinned, but shrugged. "I could hike and run and backpack for long distances without getting tired, which made me great at mapping out long geologic features and contacts. The military saw me as an inexhaustible soldier. So I joined up that summer."

Mack didn't add his choice to re-up his service for another term came when his sister Tricia disappeared. He didn't like to think on the memories his parents telling him she'd vanished out of a Las Vegas casino parking garage as if she'd never been. He'd used his contacts to find any scrap of evidence on where she'd gone, but nothing came to light.

Until he'd joined SNAIFU and received the security tape of the parking garage and the white haired, *horned*, man carrying Tricia away. He'd spent the last few years taking every weird assignment the military threw at him in an attempt to find out more about the horned man.

Yeah, with no damned luck.

"How'd you get roped into looking for me? Was it because my father is a senator?"

Mack didn't think she could pack any more venom into her questions.

"Yeah, that's about the size of it."

"I'm sorry. I wasn't running away, no matter what they told you. I just needed time to think of a way out of my father's designs. Turns out I went a little farther than expected."

Mack chuckled. "Farther is a good word for it." He shook his head. "Are you sure it's not personal?"

"Yes. Nothing personal. Kid yourself all you want, but my father does nothing without intent of his own personal gain. He already publicly announced my engagement to Coolidge with a wedding before the election. He stands to lose the large campaign contributions from the Family Focus Foundation if it doesn't come to pass."

Mack leaned his head against the wall. "He seemed pretty anxious to get you back."

"You know what they say in those cop shows? Follow the money." Bethany's hand tightened into a fist on his chest. "You do know John Coolidge is a member of the Family Focus Foundation, right?"

"No. Coolidge wasn't on our intel list. We're strictly rescue and retrieval."

"Yeah, well, here's another little tidbit I bet he didn't share. If I marry before I turn thirty, my new husband gets control of my trust fund left by my maternal grandfather. Guess what my next birthday is?"

"Thirty."

"Yep."

Mack's loathing for Coolidge increased. "So, Coolidge wants to marry you to snag the money?"

"Oh, yes, but wait. There's more. Daddy wants Coolidge to marry me because Coolidge is his stooge. Daddy can't touch the money at all. It's mine or my husband's. Granddaddy was very specific. Apparently Daddy's money lust came out early enough for Granddaddy to notice."

"Your father wants the money your grandfather set aside for you. That's sick."

"That's politics. Besides, the way he figures it, it's wasted on a woman who wants nothing more than to play with animals." Her voice held no inflection, but her shoulders tightened under Mack's arm.

"What about your mom? Didn't she have anything to say about it?"

"She died in a car accident a few years ago. That why my granddaddy's will stipulated the money had to go to me or my husband."

"I'm sorry." Mack wished he could offer her more than words.

"Thank you." Bethany sighed and squirmed a little to get more comfortable. "Now what do we do?"

"Figure out how to get out of here."

"I'm not going back to Kentucky."

"And I'm not going to leave you here."

A low vibration transferred from her to him. *Damn, is*

she actually growling at me?

"Let's try a compromise. I'll let you take me back to our home world, however we do that, as long as you don't take me back to Kentucky. Deal?"

Mack pretended to think it over. He'd definitely get them home, he just couldn't promise it wouldn't be to Kentucky. "Yeah, okay."

"Shake on it." She pulled back from him and held up her hand.

Mack hoped he wore his best poker face when he grasped her work-roughened palm in his. She might be a senator's daughter, but she no longer seemed like a spoiled princess. He hated to lie to her, but he'd be damned before he got hung out to try by her father.

"Don't shake unless you mean it." Intelligence and political savvy filled her hazel eyes.

He prayed she couldn't read minds as he gently shook her hand, mentally crossing his fingers.

"Fine. Now, how are we going to get out of here?"

"I'm working on it."

Mack scanned the walls of the stockade. They rose taller than the centaurs he'd encountered so far and while he could jump, the tops had been sharpened to points. With nothing to grab and no footholds, they'd be hard pressed to get out that way.

"For now, let's wait to see what opportunities present themselves." Mack squeezed her gently as a shiver ran through her frame. "We might have a better idea of things when the centaurs come for us."

"Fine with me. I'm freezing."

He chaffed her arms with his hands. "I'll keep you warm." Too bad it wouldn't be in the usual way. *Not that I'm interested in that. Heh.*

They lapsed into silence as he wrapped his arms around her and Mack took advantage of the downtime and increasing darkness to doze. Bethany's even breathing

90

calmed him more than he liked, but he couldn't argue with rest after the day he'd had.

The day progressed with the rain stopping only briefly. Someone brought them food and Mack only woke because the gate clanged shut and Bethany rose to retrieve the food before it got soaked.

"Thought of a way out of here yet?" Bethany handed him a thick piece of bread with butter slathered on it.

"No, not yet. Nice of the general to make you wait."

"You didn't exactly make it easy for me. They were already suspicious of humans when I showed up." She held up her hand when he opened his mouth to protest. "That wasn't an accusation, merely stating facts. There seem to be some pretty big fears surrounding mythical beasts. General Warrick might be a little more enlightened—although I'm starting to wonder—but his village is pretty stuck in the superstitious phase. He has to appear to take everyone's worries seriously or lose face."

Mack snorted. "You don't really present much of a threat."

"Do you think you could say that with a little less contempt?" Bethany shook her head as she ate what looked like a slice of apple. "Satyrs don't look particularly threatening either, but they are one of the dangerous mythological dwellers. Right up there with sirens."

"The seductive women of the sea who lure sailors onto the rocks and to their deaths?"

"Yep. Beautiful until you get up close. Then they let you flail around in panic until you drown." Bethany grimaced. "Not very nice. But they look beautiful, charming, and harmless."

"You think the centaurs are connecting you with sirens?"

"I think they're connecting me with the unknown, and most people don't deal well with that, whether they're human or centaurian."

91

Mack couldn't argue her point. He'd been sent after her because of the fear of the unknown. He recalled Stanton's words about rescue in the name of national security. *Yeah, right. More like in the name of financial security.*

They finished the meal and settled in to wait for the centaurs to come around. Bethany might not look particularly threatening, but he'd started to see why she might be more than the centaurs bargained for. Her observations of the centaurs and of their situation made him respect her more than when he'd first arrived.

The sky grew dark as the sun set and Mack settled back into sleep again. With Bethany snuggled up beside him, they stayed warm enough, but his sleep remained fitful from discomfort.

Slumber took him deep and his mind filled with strange images of the creatures he'd seen before the centaurs caught them. But while the images seemed confused at first, they all evened out into golden bronze hair and hazel eyes. Bethany's visage smiled at him with coy seduction and one of her hands caressed his chest in invitation.

Mack's cock responded with admirable alacrity and her other hand found his aching length, teasing it with feather-light touches. She wore nothing but her plaid flannel shirt unbuttoned to her breastbone and he wanted to trace her mid-line with his tongue.

"You're so hot, Mack." Her breath caressed his cheek, followed by her lips. "You're my kind of sexy."

And she was his, but some part of his mind balked at the continued fantasy. *It's just a dream.* Bethany threw back her head and laughed, her breasts jiggling under her shirt.

It could be real. The hopeful, horny part of him wanted to argue, to defend the lovely vision.

Like hell it is. Cold practicality shattered the dream as the stockade gate crashed open.

Mack jerked into consciousness and scrambled to his feet, unceremoniously dumping Bethany onto the ground.

He wanted to apologize, but he lost all his words as the largest centaur he'd ever seen stalked toward them, an ugly scowl creasing his face in the morning light.

"You are not welcome here, human."

In terms of impossible things, a huge scowling centaur ranked right up there with Santa Claus and midnight sunshine. Unfortunately for Mack the last two didn't stand around eight feet tall with hands the size of platters ready to kick his ass.

"Yeah, I got that already." Mack reached for Bethany, but never looked away from the—man? Horseman? *Whatever.*

The centaur turned his gaze on Bethany as she clambered to her feet, brushing herself off. "Mare Bethany, what is the meaning of this?" He gestured at Mack.

Bethany raised her chin and stared the centaur down. "What is the meaning of *this*?" She pointed at the stockade. "I was your Lead Mare's guest."

"And as her guest, you must abide by our rules."

"What rules have I broken?"

"You've endangered the centaurs by bringing more humans here to our world."

"I've done nothing of the sort, General." She crossed her arms over her chest, pushing up her breasts and Mack admired both the view and her tenacity. "Major McMacken came in a rescue attempt to get me home, thereby to reducing the number of humans in your midst. However, before we could continue our negotiations, we were treated like common criminals without due process." She conveniently left out her part in refusing to go with him.

Bethany's words made the general's glower deepen.

"Under the military code of justice in the Herds, we deserve a hearing."

Mack gaped. Did she just tell a bad-ass centaur general he hadn't followed his own rules of military conduct? *Damn, this woman's got balls.*

The general didn't move, but his guards shifted their weight and swished their tails in agitation. Mack got the feeling women didn't talk back much in their society.

"Very well, Mare Bethany. You shall have your hearing."

"And a bath."

"What?"

"Don't push your luck, Ms. Stanton." Mack braced for the centaur's wrath.

"I will not stand for a hearing if I cannot present myself in the best possible light. Major McMacken and I require time to bathe before we attend." Bethany ignored him, her back straight and her attitude determined. He'd kept his pistol, but she'd made it clear she didn't want him use it.

The seconds ticked by as the general glowered, but Bethany stood firm, her expression patient. Mack braced for action when the centaur growled—*Can horses make that noise?*—and tossed an order over his shoulder.

"Prepare the baths for Mare Bethany and the human male."

"Thank you, General."

"You are nearing the end of my generosity, Mare Bethany."

"Why, General?" Bethany raised her eyebrows. "I've done nothing wrong."

"The hearing shall prove or disprove that perspective."

"We shall see." She tilted her head. "It all depends on how willing you are to embrace the changes you said you wanted."

The general whuffed like an affronted stallion and pivoted, presenting them with his tail and powerful hindquarters. Mack had no illusions of the damage they could inflict if he got too close.

"My men will escort you to the facilities, Mare Bethany, and I suggest you make good use of your time. The hearing will convene after the morning meal."

"Thank you, General."

Mack watched the horse-man walk out, his back stiff. "Damn, Ms. Stanton. I'm impressed."

"Don't be. He and I were friends before you showed up."

"Friends?" Mack scowled. "Is that a euphemism?"

"What?" Bethany matched his scowl. "Eww! No, Major, we were not involved romantically. I don't think it's even physiologically possible." She shuddered. "He has his own herd of mares he presides over, and he was having trouble with his Lead Mare." She glanced at the weapon he still had in his possession. "What are we going to do with that? I have no idea where they'll take us after the trial."

Mack considered as the centaurs waited outside the stockade for them. "Let's bury it in the straw here. I can always sneak back to get it if they let us go."

She swallowed hard, biting her bottom lip, but nodded. "Okay. I'll distract the guards to keep their attention off you. Just be quick."

Mack nodded as she headed for the gate of the stockade, calling for the guards attention. He had no idea what she told them, but he found a depression in the ground beneath the straw and tucked his gear there. He spread the straw over the hiding place, hoping it looked undisturbed, and straightened as if stretching out his kinks.

Yeah, good luck with that. Those kind of kinks don't get stretched out.

"Major, are you ready?" Bethany called to him as he reached over his head to stretch his shoulders.

"Yeah, yeah. On my way." He joined her and tried to think of something to throw off any curiosity the guards might have. "Tell me more about the Lead Mare. What is the problem with her and the general?"

Bethany took a deep breath. "It's a problem that plagues male/female interactions everywhere I've been." She glanced at him with a little frown and he swore she debated saying more. "The problem is the males don't see the females as people."

Mack frowned. "What do you mean?"

"It's hard to explain, but the stallions seem to think of the mares as only female, not as people they respect for their abilities or skills. And the stallions treat the mares accordingly. As far as I can tell, the mares had started to reject the stallions' lack of respect before I arrived. The centaurs live in harem units, so more wives you have, the higher your status in the centaur world. The lead mare acts as a first wife sort of thing, and the other mares follow her lead."

"Do wives equate prestige and power?"

"Pretty much, yes."

"So they're more like possessions than companions."

Bethany considered as the guards formed up around them. "Something like that. The problem lies in the mares being treated as tradable commodities. Not very good for healthy intimate relationships. I suggested maybe the general treat his wives like, oh I don't know, people, and see how that worked out for him."

Mack barked a laugh. "You gave a centaur general relationship advice?"

"No...well, yeah. Wouldn't you rather be treated like a person, human male?"

Her use of the general's parting words drove home her point. "You wouldn't have to deal with that if you were home, Ms. Stanton."

Bethany coughed. "You're kidding, right? Have you met my father? He considers women only useful in how they appear and how malleable they are. His only interest in getting me home is marrying me off to his smarmy protégé so he can get to my inheritance." She shook her head. "I'm better off with the centaurs."

Mack couldn't think of anything to say. John Coolidge epitomized sleaze and Senator Stanton would never make his list of trustworthy men. Mack had never agreed with the traditional chauvinistic view on women. Especially after working with First Sergeant Bryant. Her body shape had never impeded her skill set. Deadly was an understatement for his NCO.

Get your head back in the game.

The centaurs led them out of the stockade and Mack scanned the grounds of the settlement for any break in ranks. While he'd left his gear in the stockade, escape remained his ultimate objective. Unfortunately, the horsemen had him outnumbered twenty to one and none of them looked like they slacked in their duties. Bethany glanced at him and sighed.

"Don't try it, Major. They're fast, big, and well-trained. Just come with me and take a bath."

He knew what she meant, but the idea of taking a bath *with* her made him grin.

"Not like that. Stop being the typical male. Could you try to rise above my expectations?"

"Which expectations are those? That I'm rugged and tough? Or that I rescue you from this nightmare?"

Bethany snorted. "Those are your expectations, not mine. This challenge won't be won with force. You're going to have to use intellect and negotiation this time."

"How can you be so sure? You've never met anyone like me." Certainly not with experiences of the weird he'd gathered. Centaurs counted as the biggest beings he'd run across, but not the strangest.

"Special forces, military, and alpha-sure-of-himself. Been there, done that, got the t-shirt, several times." She waved to the horse soldiers all around them. "And now they come horse-sized." Bethany shot him a knowing look. "Just take a bath and relax a little. We're going to have to talk our way out of this and use logic, not violence." A half smile curled her lips. "Men pride themselves on being far more logical than women, right? Show me your stuff, big guy."

Logically, we'd be better off if we'd left when I first met you.

He opened his mouth to make a wise-crack about his stuff, but she held up a hand.

"Just don't."

Mack firmed his mouth against his grin and followed their escort to a large open-sided pavilion housing a steaming pool some fifty feet across. Large benches and terraces had been built in slatted and stained wood to provide lounging spaces for beings larger than himself.

"Wow."

"Magnificent, isn't it?"

Magnificent was an understatement. The bath smelled like the jasmine flowers his mother had planted in her garden the last summer Mack lived in California. Some of his tension flowed away before he even set a foot in the steaming water. But all of his earlier excitement returned as Bethany pulled off her shirt.

"What are you doing?" *What am I doing?*

"Taking a bath. You know, hot water, soap? Any of this ringing a bell?" She arched a brow as she stripped her jeans from her legs. Smooth legs that went on for miles.

"You sure?"

"This is the one chance you have to get clean before the centaurs come back to take us to the hearing. What are you quibbling about?" Bethany turned away to unclip her bra and Mack damn near swallowed his tongue.

"There are no changing rooms."

"Wow, you're quick, Major. You've been in the military how long?" Bethany pulled her underwear off her sleek buttocks and stepped into the water. "Think of this as a campaign where you don't get to stay in a five star hotel where your delicate sensibilities are considered. And please don't tell me you've never seen a naked woman. I'd be terribly disappointed." She turned to face him, the tops of her breasts bobbing in the water. "Or are you afraid of showing your body to a woman? Worried you won't compare to the big burly centaur males who only wear leather vests?"

Aw, hell, no. She did not just taunt him with body issues. He pulled his shirt out of his pants and unzipped his field vest as a smile curled his lips. "Not one of my fears, Ms. Stanton. Unless you go for guys with a few more limbs and a lot more hair than I have." He dropped the vest on the wooden floorboards and jerked his shirt over his head, exposing his chest.

Granted, his body wasn't smooth as a baby's ass, but he couldn't be considered a hairball. Not when compared to the furred bodies of the men roaming around the bathing pavilion. But while he did have muscles necessary for a combat veteran, he wasn't nearly as ripped as the men carrying spears the diameter of a baseball bat. *Why the hell do I care how I compare to these guys?*

Bethany had already soaped up her hair and currently scrubbed her arms above the water surface. He turned his back before his cock rose in salute to the tops of her creamy breasts bobbing in the warm liquid. *Too late.* He submerged as quickly as possible, wetting down his own hair.

The discomfort of shared nudity gave way to relief and pleasure of the hot water surrounding his body. He scrubbed his own limbs and reveled in the sensation of getting clean. And relaxing. Despite their guards, they remained alone in the baths and some of the tension left Mack's shoulders.

"Feel better?"

Bethany's voice carried over the steaming water and he found her scrubbing her head with something resembling pale slime.

"I was until I saw your hair. What is that?"

She laughed and dunked her head backwards, her breasts

arching out of the water as she rinsed. Mack damn near forgot to breathe as he watched, his gaze glued to her chest.

"It's the centaur version of conditioner."

"What?"

"The slime in my hair. It's conditioner." She tilted her head and a smug smile quirked her lips. "You don't even know what I'm talking about right now, do you?"

"What you're talking about?" He knew he'd repeated her words stupidly, but his brain had gone straight to his cock and coherency was the first casualty.

"Perhaps we should begin again, Major. Do you want any soap for your bath or do you just want to bob there with your mouth open?"

He snapped his mouth shut so fast his teeth clacked and he dunked his head in hopes of washing away his chagrin. *Holy shit, I'm thirty-six years old and acting like a fuckin' teenager.* When he came back up, Bethany laughed and handed him a cake of soap. The scent reminded him of his favorite bakery growing up when the old baker would make rosemary bread. He accepted the soap and scrubbed everything he could reach without showing too much.

Bethany turned her back, but not before a knowing grin stretched her lips. He swallowed a mutter about minxes and scrubbed his unruly body with the savory soap. Splashing distracted him and he turned just in time to smack his hand into Bethany's shoulder. Unfortunately, he released the soap into the water.

"Oh, no. Grab that." Bethany swiped at the slippery bar, but it squirted out of her grasp and skimmed across the water.

They both dove after it in an attempt to catch it, but ended up tangled in each other. The bar sank beneath their combined wave and Bethany sank after it, squealing as he followed her down. Soft, warm wet skin slid along his limbs, and he tried to pull her back out of the water. But she squirmed too far to one side and he lost his balance, laughing as he fell with a large splash.

Bethany stood up, the water sluicing off her breasts and belly as she held her hair away from her face. She twisted and turned, looking through the churning water for the soap, and he couldn't remember anything quite so beautiful.

"Where is it? Where's the soap?"

Mack peered into the water around him, but saw nothing but the light reflections on the chop.

"You lost it!" Her voice sounded accusatory, but her grin spoiled the affect.

"Me? You're the one who knocked it out of my hand." He tried to frown, but her grin was too infectious. He stalked toward her, skimming his hands over the surface, trying to settle the water.

"I just wanted to see if you were done with it." She shook her head, spraying droplets of water around her like a fan. "Now it's on the bottom somewhere."

"What's the big deal? It's hot water. It'll dissolve the soap and dilute it." He stopped beside her and looked down, ostensibly scanning for the cake of soap. *And if I happen to notice her nipples are golden brown just like her bush, that's just incidental, right?*

"Yeah, but it's my favorite soap and the only cake I have." Bethany turned toward him and he hastily turned away before the slit in his cock greeted her above the water's shifting surface. *Nothing like showing off.*

A resigned sigh preceded the sounds of her leaving the pool and he had the pleasure of watching the water sluice silvery trails down her curvaceous body. Damn, senator's daughter or not, Bethany Stanton would star in his midnight fantasies for years after this mission.

She strode over to a small table stacked with towels and wrapped herself in one before turning back to the pool with another. Mack had never been so envious of terry cloth in his life.

"Here. Are you ready?"

"Ready?" He still had trouble following her conversation. *Now, following the droplets between her breasts...*

"To get out. We probably don't have much time before they call the trial." Bethany held up the extra towel. "I'm sure the centaurs would be delighted to see you naked and dripping wet, but you might feel more comfortable dressed while facing them."

A cold splash of reality brought Mack around. That's right, she's arranged a trial. Any arousal he felt looking at Bethany dissolved in the thought of a tribunal. Not quite a court-martial, but it could still end up in death. He rose out of the water and wrapped the towel around his waist before striding to the others to dry the rest of him. "Do you think they left me any clean clothes?"

CHAPTER NINE

Bethany swallowed hard and tried not to think of the Major with all those glorious, glistening muscles outlined in wet hair. *Good Lord, he's prettier than a group of SEALs on PT.* She pretended to ignore how his body flexed as he dried himself off, and she did *not* remember size and shape of his penis and testicles when he emerged from the water.

No, not at all.

With his back turned, she could see the scars and marks of his experience, and something about them warmed her heart as well as turned her on. This man hadn't gotten his body merely being a gym-rat, although she suspected he worked out enough. He'd used his body helping others, defending those who needed him, and fighting what needed to be fought.

What is wrong with me? I'm not a fan of military men. They're arrogant as hell and rarely come home. She shook her head to clear it of the fogging attraction.

"Bethany?"

"What, hmm?" She blinked and tried to figure out what he'd asked.

"Do you think they left me any clean clothes?"

"Why would you need more clothes?" She wished she

could take it back the moment she said it, and tried to cover with snarkiness. "I mean, isn't part of the military prowess showing off as much of your muscular strength as you can?"

Mack shook his head and chuckled. "Maybe in our world. But I don't think my bipedal physique would impress those with six limbs."

"Remember, strength and limb number isn't everything." She grinned and he laughed. "I think they left us both some robes. I know the sewing team found my need to cover most of my body odd, but perhaps they translated that to you for breeches and tunic."

"Good. I don't really want to wear a skirt."

"Neither do I." She gave him a dry look that morphed into her best mock-innocence. "You wouldn't wear a kilt? The Irish do it often enough, and McMacken is Irish, isn't it?"

He narrowed his eyes and tilted his head. "Are ye suggesting I'm not real Irish if I don't choose to wear me kilt?"

His lovely lilting accent caught Bethany off-guard and her belly fluttered in feminine appreciation.

"You do that very well, Major. Where'd you learn the accent?"

"'Twas part o' me training in the military, it was." He hammed it up as he scrubbed his hair. "And you can call me Mack like me friends do."

"Mack?"

"Yeah." He dropped the accent and searched the baths for clothing. "Less formal than Major, and more to the point than McMacken."

She followed him around the baths as he searched for clothing, enjoying the way the muscles in his back flexed as he walked. She counted ten scars and wondered how he healed from each. Sometimes the outer marks served as a warning to inner scars, but Mack didn't act shut off from the world. *What do I know? I've talked to him for about twenty-four hours.* Not exactly a lifetime.

"Ah, here we go. Do you think the green and brown stuff is for me?"

Bethany laughed and nodded. "The males prefer to blend in with their surroundings, especially when at war." She picked up the peachy-sunset colored tunic with a V-neck embroidered in red and gold. "Besides, I'm not sure V-necks are quite your style."

She dropped her towel and slid the tunic over her head until it settled on her shoulders. It draped to her knees, but hugged her body well enough to show her feminine curves. When she looked up, she found Mack watching her, his expression intense, but unreadable.

"What?"

"Uh, sorry." He shook his head like a dog clearing itself of water. "So the green tunic goes over the brown pants?" He held them up. "It's a little big."

Big was an understatement. The shoulders of the tunic stretched beyond his by a good six inches, and the hem hung to nearly his ankles. Fortunately, the slits up the sides allowed for movement. The pants draped too short, but at least they fit his trim waist.

"I think they mirrored the pants after mine." Bethany held them up to Mack's hips in front of the towel. "Um, I'm not sure they're cut for..."

"For?"

"For extra body." She showed him the front. "See? Flat seams. That means I can wear them, but anyone with male equipment might be hard-pressed. So to speak."

He held up the pants to look and scowled. "Looks like I'm wearing a kilt after all, lassie."

Bethany couldn't help but smile. "At least they gave you a sash to keep the tunic close to your waist. You'll still show a lot of leg, but I think hairy legs are sexy on men."

Mack raised an eyebrow and his lips quirked as Bethany

wondered where the hell that had come from. She shouldn't be thinking of Major McMacken in terms of sexy. She had to get her head in the game and be ready for the trial.

"Good thing. I wasn't going to shave them any time soon."

She laughed and hoped he didn't notice how her nipples tightened with his cheeky smile. *He's military, remember?* For some reason, she couldn't get past his humor and good looks, and she fiercely repeated his rank in her head as they finished dressing.

"Wow."

Bethany looked up. "What?"

"That's beautiful." He grimaced as he waved at her clothes. "I mean, you're beautiful in them."

The tunic looked much like his, but tailored for a female shape. It reminded her of something she'd seen women wearing in India, except it had a sash for her waist instead of a stole or scarf.

"Thanks, I think."

"Oh, it was meant as a compliment."

His words warmed her insides more than she liked and she turned away to use a comb for her hair. Without accessories, she could do little more than tie it in a knotted bun, but at least it looked somewhat professional. *As if I know what that is in this world.*

Mack cleared his throat behind her. "Ready?"

She glanced over her shoulder and noted his hands curled into tight fists against his thighs.

"Yes. Are you okay?"

"Yeah. I'm good." He nodded sharply and turned his gaze toward the figures of the centaurs milling outside the baths. "Let's get this show on the road."

Bethany raised her chin, took a deep breath, and resumed the "senator's-daughter" mask she often wore to public functions. She'd never gone to law school, but she'd be acting as her own lawyer today. *What's that line about a man being his own lawyer having a fool for a client?* She swallowed her nervousness and hoped she wasn't a fool. *Like I have a lot of choice.*

They emerged from the heat of the baths into the weak autumn sunshine and Bethany took a deep breath. The air smelled of fallen leaves baking in the sun and an odd scent unique to centaurs. Not quite sweat and not quite horse, but something in between. *At least it's not manure.*

"Mare Bethany, you and the human male will follow us to the Hall of Elders." One of the big centaur guards gestured imperiously toward the center of the village.

Bethany nodded, saving her energy for the trial to come. Mack fell in beside her, his bearing still relaxed.

"It's great to be identified by my species and gender." He scowled.

"Be grateful they didn't call you my pet."

He glanced at her with a raised eyebrow. "Should I start panting and slavering at the mouth?"

"If you think it will help." Bethany patted his arm at his frown. "Look, they understand men and military. They're trying to break you down before they even get out the big guns. Didn't you ever watch any lawyer shows on TV? Most trials are won by flustering the witnesses or defendants. Just put on your soldier's face and wear your mental body armor." She squeezed the hard muscle under her hand before letting go. "Think you can do that?"

He tilted his head as they neared the Hall of Elders. "How do you know so much about military men when you choose to avoid them?"

"My brother is a Navy SEAL." She shrugged. "He was a master of not letting my father's insults get to him. I figure you can't be too much different."

"I've never been prone to rising to bait." He squared his shoulders and lost all expression from his face.

"Let's hope you're right."

The centaurs ushered them through the doors of the Hall

and herded them into the center of an open area lit by sunshine. The rest of the hall sat in shadow, so the interrogators could see the accused well, but not the other way around. Two low-walled enclosures about seven feet long and four feet wide stood in the light, the boards coming up to Bethany's chest. The guards shoved her into one and Mack into the other, closing the gate behind her. She had plenty of room, but suspected the structures would make a centaur uncomfortable.

Bethany shielded her eyes to scan the edges of the Hall and found General Warrick and the other elders reclining on specially made chairs to support their equine bodies. *Great, they'll be able to sit here all day. Let's hope they're not that patient.* A low murmur filled the hall as the elders spoke among themselves, but Bethany kept her gaze on Warrick. His opinion mattered most in this tribunal. Not only did he have the most pull, but he knew her best.

The click of locks on the gates of their stalls made Bethany share a glance with Mack. If need be, they'd easily climb over the sides and break for the door. *Let's hope it doesn't come to that.* Mack nodded and turned to face the tribunal. *At least we're on the same page there.*

"Let us open this trial in the name of the Lady Epona. Sweet Goddess, hear our prayers. Grant us the clarity to see the truth in all that transpires here today."

Bethany recognized the speaker as Stal Corbin, the older centaur who'd tried to grab her on the day of her arrival. He met her gaze with a smug sneer, evidently pleased to see her on trial. *I hope his manipulations of this situation don't carry much weight.*

"He looks like he has it in for you." Mack's low voice reached her ears though he kept his face forward.

"He isn't my biggest fan."

"What did you do to him?"

"Nothing." Bethany raised her chin. "He blames me for the female centaurs refusing to be treated as possessions."

"Mare Bethany, you stand accused of endangering the Forest Edge clan by bringing in more odd human invaders. How do you plead?"

"Not guilty." Bethany met Warrick's gaze without flinching.

"The human beside you would suggest the contrary."

"It's the truth." Bethany shrugged.

Warrick's lips tightened and he narrowed his eyes. "Very well. State your name, species, and occupation for this tribunal."

"Bethany Stanton, human, and I'm a veterinarian, a healer of horses."

Mack leaned toward her. "I thought vets worked on all animals."

"We all have specialties, don't we, Major?" Bethany kept her gaze locked on Warrick.

"Yes, we do."

Why the hell did that confidence warm her chest? *Let it go, Stanton. Focus.*

"Please give your account of your actions yesterday morning."

Bethany nodded, taking a deep breath as she flattened her hands on the railing of the wood enclosure. She wanted to pace, just like the lawyers in the TV shows, but she didn't have the luxury.

"As you know, three weeks ago I arrived in the sacred grove of the dryads by way of the Rift between my world and yours. At that time, I'd been unaware such a doorway existed." She shot a look at Mack, but he didn't meet her eyes. "I was immediately taken into custody by Captain Yarren Plainsrunner and brought here to the Forest Edge clan's village, where General Warrick Spearthrower dictated the terms of my residency."

"What were those terms, Mare Bethany?" one of the other elder's asked.

"I was required to negotiate a new understanding

between General Warrick Spearthrower and Lead Mare Idrissa Plainsrunner in an effort to restore harmony among the mares and stallions of the clan."

Mack whistled low between his teeth. "Damn."

Bethany held back a grimace. It hadn't been a picnic.

"How would you characterize these negotiations, Mare Bethany?"

"Difficult and arduous." Bethany shrugged. "Centaurs in general are a determined and confident species. Both the mares and the stallions are so certain they know what's right. There have been mistakes made on both sides and both camps are entrenched in their beliefs. Neither have been willing to compromise or bend in their view of the situation."

"This is because stallions are and have always been the leaders." Stal Corbin leveled an angry look at her. "There is no disputing this."

"The mares don't dispute this, either, Stal. However, their complaints lie in their treatment as less than a full centaur, nothing more than vessels for sexual congress and maintaining the home and herd." Bethany ignored the similarities to her own world.

"You've stirred them up. Because of you, they're no longer treating with us." The older centaur's nostrils widened and a fierce scowl marred his face.

"I have not. I've only done what General Warrick has asked of me in accordance to my residency terms." Bethany kept her voice even. She'd played this game enough times in her father's house and remembered how to dismantle someone with stoicism. Her father had done it to many people over the years.

"Continue, Mare Bethany." Warrick waved for her to move on, his lips tightening with annoyance. "Let's get to the incident of yesterday morning."

Bethany nodded, amused by Warrick's discomfort. "Yesterday morning, I left the village to find some peace from the ongoing negotiations. Both parties were being intractable and I'd run out of ideas of how to reach an accord." The frustration with both Lead Mare Idrissa and Warrick still simmered in the back of Bethany's mind. "I'd walked to the edge of the forest to find some clarity of thought. My intentions were to determine something the two parties could compromise on. Something that would give each the majority of their demands."

Bethany slid her gaze over the tribunal. Each wore a variation of disbelief or disapproval. She resisted the urge to stick her tongue out at them. *Pompous bastards.*

"While going over the issues, I encountered a satyr."

Mack grunted. "So that's what it was."

"As I'm sure you're all aware, satyrs are manipulative and beguiling." Murmurs of assent rippled through the elders. "I would've succumbed to its charms had Major McMacken not arrived."

"You mean, been summoned." Stal Corbin scowled.

"No, arrived. It was my understanding from this body of authority that the rift to my world was closed." Bethany raised her chin. "I had no expectation of returning to my world, nor that anyone would arrive from it. As far as my understanding went, I would remain in the village for the unforeseen future."

She swung her gaze to the others. "Major McMacken informed me he intended to return me to my homeworld and I insisted there was no way to get back. He then attempted to force me back to the sacred grove, and I resisted because he didn't see the signs."

"Which signs?" General Warrick frowned.

"The signs of the dryads' response to those who defile or abuse their lands. I'd encountered the princess lamp on my arrival and didn't wish the same fate. That's when I called for General Warrick and the others."

"Are you saying this human came without your special instructions and meant to return you to your home through the rift without your permission?"

"That's exactly what I'm saying. I neither invited nor expected Major McMacken's presence, and as far as I was concerned, had no expectation of the rift being open again." She shot a look at Mack. "However, he informed me he'd only been in this world for three days, while I've been here three weeks. You can imagine my surprise to find out the rift had been open this long."

"It's not open." An elder centaur with braided dreds and cocoa-colored skin spoke up. "We've checked and rechecked the celestial alignments as well as scanned the sacred grove for energy surges. Everything has been quiet." He leveled her with a scowl. "I assure this tribunal, the rift is closed."

"It wasn't closed. I came through just as Ms. Stanton reported," Mack said.

"Be quiet, human. You've not been given permission to speak."

Oh, yeah, that should work on him. Mack's expression settled into impassiveness, but his shoulders tensed and his hands coiled into fists at his sides.

"Have you anything to add to this testimony, Mare Bethany?" A third Elder with snowy-white hair cut short like a Marine's dipped his chin.

"Only that while I've been here, I've done nothing to endanger the village, nor have I come close to the sacred grove until the morning I met Major McMacken."

"What were your duties while in the village, Mare Bethany?" Warrick seemed to be prompting her despite his role as a member of the tribunal.

"I was asked to facilitate a negotiation between General Warrick and Lead Mare Idrissa."

"Did you perform any other tasks during your negotiations?" Stal Corbin sneered.

"Yes."

Warrick's mouth twitched as if smothering a smile.

Corbin scowled. "Can you elaborate?"

"I helped heal small injuries to the mares in General Warrick's household, patching cuts and scrapes. Lead Mare Idrissa asked me to keep her sister mares in good health."

"How did you know how to care for centaurs when you claim to know nothing about them?"

"I used the collective wisdom of the mares to accentuate the accumulated learning I have with regards to horses and women in my own world." Bethany crossed her arms over her chest. "Two things I know pretty well, Stal. Horses and women."

Corbin glowered, but Warrick snorted. "Do you have anything else to add?"

"Only that while I stayed in the village, I've done no harm, and yet when General Warrick and the others came to my aid, I was summarily accused of endangering the village, arrested, and thrown in the stockade without due process." Bethany lifted her chin and stared at the tribunal. "I wasn't aware your way of dealing with those suspected of wrong-doing was guilty-until-proven-innocent. I've since amended my understanding."

Mack hissed a warning at her side, but she stood her ground. *No good deed goes unpunished.* Bethany had just about enough of males of any species treating her as less than human. Or less than centaurian in this case. If she'd done something heinous throughout the three weeks she'd been there, it would make sense. But she'd done nothing.

The centaur with the jarhead haircut cleared his throat and glanced at the others before speaking. "Very well. If there's nothing else you can add, we'll now hear testimony from Lead Mare Idrissa with regards to Mare Bethany's conduct in the village."

Corbin scowled. "What could the Lead Mare offer? She's just a female."

Bethany dropped her hands to her sides before the centaurs caught sight of the fists she wanted to use to pummel the old misogynist.

"Have a care, Stal Corbin, when speaking of my Lead Mare." General Warrick's expression darkened. "Female or not, she's more than earned the respect of this council and this village." He gestured to the guards. "Please show the Lead Mare in."

Some of the tension drained from Bethany's shoulders. Warrick had never defended Idrissa in any of the conversations she'd witnessed, and she had hope this boded well for their negotiations. *If I make it out of here unscathed.*

CHAPTER TEN

Mack watched the guards lead in a female centaur with the regal bearing of a queen and the air to match. The woman had charcoal gray hair, but it matched the stockings and tail of her horse portion, and didn't appear to be from age. Diaphanous sleeves fluttered from wrist and shoulder as she swung her arms, and golden bangles encircled her wrists and fetlocks. He found her human portion beautiful and had to give Warrick kudos for his choice in Lead Mare.

"Welcome, Lead Mare. Please state your name, species, and occupation for this tribunal." The centaur who reminded Mack of an old Marine nodded to her.

"My name is Idrissa Plainsrunner, I'm a centaur, and I'm Lead Mare to the Forest Edge clan." She crossed her arms under her ample breasts held by a pale purple half-shirt connected to the sleeves at the shoulders. Mack tried not the stare at her chest.

"Thank you, Lead Mare. Please tell this tribunal what you know of Mare Bethany and her conduct in the village."

The regal woman inclined her head as she gathered her thoughts. A crystal-encrusted tiara winked in the light of the torches flickering inside the barn. *Talk about an old-fashioned, down-home trial*. At least no one stood around with shotguns and overalls.

"Mare Bethany is a kind, caring, and forthright guest in my household and she has done nothing beyond her duties while here in the village." Idrissa met the tribunal's gazes without tremor or fear.

The centaur called Corbin scowled. "This tells us nothing. The Lead Mare is conspiring with the human to undermine our control."

Mack ground his teeth and clenched his fists before he told the old bastard to shut up. Fortunately, he didn't have to.

"Be still, Stal Corbin. Your disdain has been noted, but this tribunal will hear the Lead Mare's testimony." The Marine centaur's voice hadn't changed pitch, but Corbin grunted as if taking a blow.

Mack stifled a smile and kept his gaze from straying anywhere.

"To your knowledge, Lead Mare, what were the duties assigned to Mare Bethany?"

"Mare Bethany was ordered to negotiate a new way of understanding between General Warrick and his mares." Idrissa glanced at Bethany before turning her gaze to the tribunal. "She has done so admirably and with great patience despite setbacks."

"Yet, has it not escalated? Aren't all the mares now protesting treatment by their males?" Corbin thumped the desk before him. "The human female is a menace and now she's brought another."

Idrissa raised an eyebrow. "Was there a question in that for me, Stal Corbin, or were you merely venting your spleen?"

Mack caught Warrick's lips twitching to hide a smile and he mentally shook his head. *Damn, that woman has moxy.*

The Marine centaur cleared his throat. "What other duties did Mare Bethany assume while in the village, Lead

116

Mare?"

"I learned Mare Bethany had healer abilities from her schooling in her own world and I asked her as my guest to use them for healing minor hurts and increasing the general health of the mares, not only in General Warrick's harem, but of the other harems in the village." Idrissa swung her gaze along the line of males listening. "With our knowledge of medicinal herbs and her skills at healing, she has improved the lives of the mares."

"And incited them to defy their stallions." Corbin's whining pissed Mack off and he took a deep breath, swallowing his need to tell the old fool to shut up.

"She neither incited them nor encouraged them to defy anyone, Stal Corbin." Idrissa fixed him with her serene expression. "She has merely reminded the mares that they are not chattel and should be treated with the respect as a living, aware being in this community. Are you saying the mares in your harem are not deserving of respect, Stal Corbin?"

"Mares should know their place!" Corbin thrust a finger at Bethany. "She incited them to defy their stallions and then brought another human into the village. Who knows what trouble he'll add?"

"Do you know this for certain, Stal Corbin?" Idrissa asked, placing her hands on either side of her human waist. "Were you privy to this information? Did you hear her planning to, as you say, "incite the mares" or to bring in more humans?" Idrissa snorted and scowled her disdain. "Mare Bethany has lived with me these three weeks and has dealt with me, the mares, and the other stallions with nothing but respect, compassion, and patience. At no time has she spoken of going home, bringing in more of her people, or undermining the order and operation of this community."

The Lead Mare shifted her weight and rested her gaze on Mack's. Wisdom, intelligence, and experience filled her steel-blue eyes as she scanned him, and Mack had the odd impression she judged whether he'd be worthy of Bethany. *What the hell?*

"I don't know what brought the other human here, but it certainly wasn't through Mare Bethany's efforts." Idrissa focused on the tribunal again. "While the presence of one's own species often brings solace, Mare Bethany has conducted herself with decorum and respect without the expectation of interaction with her own. Her behavior in the village has improved the lives of the mares and has in no way endangered this herd."

"Has she ever spoken to you about her home or the possibility of returning there?" General Warrick wore tension like a second skin and Mack wondered what bothered the centaur so much. *Either it's the answer to the question or the one answering it.*

Idrissa shook her head. "Mare Bethany only spoke of her home with regards to knowledge gained there or people she knew while around me. She never mentioned returning or suggested anyone would come after her. From all I heard, Mare Bethany intended to stay with this village and continue her work in the negotiation."

Mack shot a glance at Bethany. Why the hell wouldn't she expect rescue? *Maybe because she found herself in some fantasy world with mythical beasts? Think, jackass.*

"She's lying." Corbin's mouth settled into a sneer, malice and disdain oozing from every portion of his body language. "She only wishes to hide one of her own from justice."

This guy is spoiling for a fight. While the other members of the tribunal erupted into protests and dismay, the Lead Mare only raised her chin and met Corbin's malicious gaze with calm serenity. Mack glanced at Bethany. The senator's daughter gave nothing away, but he thought he caught a quick shake of her head in disbelief.

"Quiet!" General Warrick's shout slapped an immediate

silence over the assembled and his gaze curbed even Corbin's virulent malice. "The Lead Mare's integrity is not in question here, nor should it ever be. We are here to determine Mare Bethany's role in endangering the village." He shot a quelling look to everyone on the tribunal before swinging his gaze back to Idrissa. "Have you anything to add, Lead Mare?"

"No, General. My testimony stands as is."

"Thank you, Lead Mare. You may depart."

Mack watched the female centaur wheel away and stride toward to back of the barn, her head held high. He suspected she fumed inside, but she didn't give anything away. *That's one tough lady.* He glanced at Bethany. *Kinda like her.* Corbin didn't like either of them.

"Seems like there's some history here." Mack leaned toward Bethany as the tribunal spoke quietly amongst themselves. "Think Corbin has a bone to pick with the Lead Mare?"

Bethany shrugged. "I haven't heard anything about it. I've only been here three weeks, you know."

"What I mean is have you noticed that guy out to get you or General Warrick before?" Mack nodded at the older centaur. "He's got a burr under his saddle for you. Hell, for anything female I'd guess."

"Maybe he just doesn't like to be told no." Bethany shot Mack a significant look before facing forward once more.

"Mare Bethany, after much discussion, it appears you have not brought this other human to our village." The centaur with the jarhead haircut waved at Mack. "However, your behavior after incarceration has been brought into question."

"My behavior afterward? What do you mean, stal?"

"According to a report from the guards, you refused to hand over the male human's belongings. All prisoners of war must relinquish their gear upon capture."

"We are not at war, Stal." Bethany raised her chin, but

her expression remained relaxed. "And he'd done nothing to harm the centaurs even when they arrived. His items were his own and when I was incarcerated along with him, I didn't see a need to be cooperative with those who'd arrested me."

"Where are his belongings now?"

Mack's gut clenched and he held his breath, but Bethany shrugged. "I don't know, stal. I assumed he had them with him when we went to the baths. As you can see, we are wearing the clothing left for us."

Warrick's eyes narrowed and he opened his mouth to say something when the doors behind them slammed against the walls with a crash. Shouts and protests filled the space as a new, younger centaur galloped in, tension and panic in every line of his body. Mack listened hard for sounds of battle, but he couldn't hear anything over the shouting cacophony.

"Forgive me, General Warrick, but there's been an incident." The younger male's sides pumped like a bellows as he skidded to a halt in front of the tribunal.

"What is it, Captain? Are we being attacked?" The general shifted his weight, his hands tightening on the desk before him.

"No, worse. Mare Sonja has fallen and broken a foreleg."

Dire silence hit the room just before Mack caught movement out of the corner of his eye. Bethany vaulted over the sides of their stall enclosures and headed for the captain.

"Where is she, Captain? Is she conscious?"

For a moment, Mack thought the centaur would strike out at Bethany and he launched himself over the wall of his stall. But the captain turned pleading eyes on the woman beside him, his expression a mask of despair.

"She's conscious, Mare Bethany, but the leg is badly broken."

"Can you show me? Let me see what can be done."

"Nothing can be done." The captain shook his head. "She's cannot be helped."

Bethany laid a hand on his arm, waiting until the centaur looked at her as Mack came up behind her. "Please, Captain Yarren. Let me take a look. I only want what's best for her. There may be something I can do. As we say at home, it ain't over until the fat lady sings."

Yarren gave her a quizzical look, but he nodded before facing the tribunal once again. "Permission to take Mare Bethany to my lead mare Sonja, General."

"You are aware that Mare Bethany is on trial for endangering the village, Captain Yarren?"

Yarren nodded sharply. "I am, sir. But Mare Bethany has only treated my mares with kindness and they have spoken well of her. Against my initial assessment of the human female, she has proven to be a respectful and honorable companion to my mares."

"Oh, for goodness sake. Can we get on with this? There's a mare in trouble." Bethany gestured toward the doors.

Respectful until now. Mack suppressed his grin as he kept an eye out for anyone attempting to do harm to Bethany. He didn't trust Stal Corbin any further than he could spit, and the others were marginal in their support. While he didn't feel his most powerful in a long robe without pants, he'd be damned before he let clothing stop him from his mission.

Which is what, now? If the rift he'd come through was closed, how would they get back to their world? He shoved the thought aside. *As she said, it ain't over until the fat lady sings.*

"We haven't reached a decision about you, Mare Bethany," Jarhead said, a frown creasing his brow.

"You'll know where to find me. Captain, where is Sonja?"

Yarren scanned the tribunal for a few moments before he wheeled toward the doors. "This way, Mare Bethany."

Mack swore the centaurs behind him would explode as Bethany followed the captain outside. Mack covered her back, keeping an ear out for pursuit. This would either make or break Bethany's case, but might push up his bid to get her out of here. If the centaurs intended to punish her for his arrival, he'd take the decision out of their hands.

The wind had come up while they'd been listening to Bethany's testimony and the grasses whipped back and forth in the minor gale shaking the village. Clouds scuttled overhead as if fleeing a monster in the west and Mack looked for Bethany. She jogged beside the centaur captain, her robes flying in the increased breeze.

Mack took off after them, ignoring the thunder of hooves behind him. They passed the stockade and he made a mental note to return after dark to retrieve his gear. Centaurs watched curiously as the captain directed Bethany to a smaller stable closer to what looked like a barracks. *Captain stays near his men.* Mack approved and followed them inside the barn.

"Easy, Sonja, I'm here."

Bethany's voice caressed his ears as much as those of the female centaur lying on a couch inside the stable, tears streaming down her face. Another female centaur stood beyond her and a third held her injured sister, their faces creased with worry and sorrow.

"You're not welcome here, human."

Mack looked way up into the scowling, bearded face of the captain and tried to find some compassion for the man. "Ask me if I care, Captain. Mare Bethany is the whole reason I'm here and where she goes, I go. Humans stick together like that."

"She has been accepted by the village, human. You have not."

"Accepted, really? From what I saw in that barn, you lot

were working awfully hard to oust her." Mack met the captain's gaze despite their severe height difference. The man's expression darkened. "Look, from one soldier to another, I'd be derelict in my duty to Mare Bethany if I didn't stand by her. Take it or leave it. I'm staying."

Some of the hostility left the captain's eyes. "Mare Bethany is *your* mare?" One of the thick eyebrows rose.

Mine field! If he said yes, Bethany would give him what-for, possibly before the assembled centaurs. But if he didn't, he'd get no quarter from Yarren. Time to hedge his bet.

"Not in the traditional sense. She's under my care." He glanced at Bethany, but the woman focused on the female centaur and didn't appear to be listening. "Her...sire asked me to look after her and I gave him my word that I'd find and protect her. I can't step aside."

Yarren huffed a sigh. "Her sire is the Stallion of the herd?"

He'd like to think so. "Yes, and I'm honor-bound to stay with her." Not strictly true, but close enough for SNAIFU.

"Very well, human, you may stay. This will be a trying time for all." Yarren shifted aside.

"Thanks, Captain." Mack stepped around him and crouched beside Bethany. "How bad is it?"

"I'm done for." Sonja sobbed in the other mare's arms, tears marring the lovely heart-shaped face.

"Shh, Sonja. All will be well." The other female said the words, but her face suggested otherwise.

"Do you know anything about horses, Major?" Bethany's expression said she didn't expect so.

"Yeah, actually. I grew up around quarter horses. My family owned a cutting stable."

"Really? Then you must know my father's stable. Kentucky Blue Grass Quarter Horses."

Mack snorted. "Pretty much everyone knows that stable."

Bethany shrugged and nodded. "So if you know horses, take a look at her leg here. See how her cannon bone bends near the fetlock?" Bethany pointed to Sonja's foreleg, the white sock resting at an odd angle to the rest of her limb. "It's not a compound fracture, but I'll need to straighten and cast it."

"How will you cast it?"

"I don't know, but I'm sure the mares know how."

"There's no need for casting spells, Mare Bethany. Sonja will have to be put down." Yarren stood over them, his expression dour and Sonja sobbed harder.

"Shhh, Sonja, it's all right." Bethany laid her hand against the mare's shoulder while she leveled a dark look at Yarren. "What do you mean put down? Euthanized?"

He nodded heavily, aging several years in that moment.

"Don't be ridiculous. She doesn't need to be euthanized. She needs to have her leg casted and she'll heal just fine." Bethany rose to her feet and faced off with Yarren as the other centaurs finally caught up with them.

"That's not our way, Mare Bethany." The captain choked on his words. "Any centaur who cannot run or hunt must be sacrificed to the Goddess Epona."

Mack swore Bethany would take a swing at the stallion in her frustrated fury and he sidled closer to her. Despite the murderous look in her eyes, the senator's daughter inhaled deeply and straightened her shoulders as she raised her chin.

"Let me get this straight. If one of your warriors is injured, such as a broken leg or arm, he's immediately put to death?"

"Not for an arm injury, Mare Bethany. But broken legs are another matter." General Warrick stepped forward, his expression full of sorrow. "I'm sorry, Yarren."

"Wait, wait, wait." Bethany backed up until she stood in front of Sonja with her arms outstretched to block anyone from getting close. "She is a living member of your herd, of your household, Yarren. She can hear you and talk to you. Hell, she's smart enough to take care of herself. Give her a little credit. You can't just kill her."

"It's our way."

"To hell with your way."

"What are you doing, Bethany?" Mack stood beside her, wishing like hell he had his Glock with him as he scanned the angry centaurs.

"Defending the weak. Isn't that one of your oaths as a soldier?" She focused on the general and his captain. "Sonja can be taught how to take care of her leg. She doesn't have to die. I can set it so it heals and she'll walk again."

"Move aside, Mare Bethany." Warrick's voice held compassion as well as resignation. "She cannot run. She cannot hunt. She would easily be killed if we were attacked. It is a mercy."

"No, it's a way of relieving responsibility." Her voice cracked like a whip and all the males took a step back as she pointed at Yarren. "You claim to be her stallion, the one who protects her from danger. Right? This is the arrangement you have made to keep a herd of mares. She needs your protection now, Captain. You're family, along with your other mares." Bethany swung one hand toward to two other women near Sonja. "They can help care for her, bring her food, help rehabilitate her. Sonja is a person, your lead mare. She's smart, beautiful, and kind. I can set her leg and rig a sling. It'll take her six weeks to heal if she rests and has support. Six weeks, Captain, to save your wife, a woman who does a helluva lot more than just warm your stable."

Mack watched the centaurs, ready for anything as Bethany stood up to all of them. He had to admit she had guts and wouldn't back down. He admired her tenacity, but he didn't think she'd win this one. What was one human woman against the tradition of an entire species?

"This is what I warned against, General." The nasty, malicious voice of Stal Corbin filled the space as the older centaur pushed to the front. "The female human is in collusion with the mares. Now she's even trying to change our traditions. I told you she incited the mares to revolt. This is the last straw. Something must be done."

Aw fuck. Mack shifted his weight to both feet and braced himself for combat. Hand-to-hand would suck with no pants and no weapons, but he'd faced bad odds before. *Of course it wasn't against centaurs...Yeah, this is gonna suck.*

CHAPTER ELEVEN

Bethany stood her ground in front of Sonja as Corbin barreled toward her, his face a mask of fury and contempt. *Right back atcha, asshole.* She didn't want to be the backstop for 1500 pounds of angry centaur, but she'd be damned before she let him make her turn away from someone who needed help. The first someone who could actually ask for it.

Before Corbin could reach her, Yarren pivoted sideways and slammed his hindquarters into Corbin's abdomen just above his forelegs. The resulting collision drove the breath from Corbin's body and he went down on his knees. Bethany swallowed hard as the centaurs shouted at each other and pandemonium broke loose around them. She backed up until Sonja rested at her back and Mack stood beside her, hoping they wouldn't get trampled in the melee.

The view suddenly disappeared as Idrissa and two other mares blocked the path, their bulk shielding Bethany and Mack from the fighters. *That's probably a first for the major.* She suspected he usually stood on the front lines with his men. She glanced at him in his court finery without pants. Despite his odd dress, he looked like he could take down a few centaurs before he fell.

Bethany let the others watch her back as she crouched besides Sonja.

"How are you doing, Sonja?"

The centaur woman's eyes held tears of pain and fear, but her face remained stoic. "As well as could be, Mare Bethany."

"May I check your leg? I need to feel how bad the break is."

Sonja nodded and Bethany ran her hands over the long cannon bone. The silky white fur slid through her palms as she tested the severity of the break. She closed her eyes and let her hands tell her the news. *Feels like a clean break. Should set well.*

Sonja jerked under her touch and Bethany opened her eyes. "It's going to be all right, Sonja. I can set it and bind it. It'll heal well if you can keep it in the sling. Can you do that?"

The white blond woman met Bethany's gaze, tears still streaming. "How do you know it will heal, Mare Bethany?"

"Because I've experienced bad breaks like this when I was younger. I've seen it before." She gave Sonja a confidant smile. "A cast, a little rest, and some time, and you'll be good as new."

"Will I be able to run again?"

Bethany took a deep breath. How far could she stretch her knowledge? In her experience, horses rarely recovered, which was why they put them down. But Sonja could be reasoned with and instructed how to care for her injury. *It's essentially the metacarpal, but she has no other bones or ligaments pulling on it.* One long middle digit that could be wrapped and secured long enough to heal.

"Yes, with proper food, rest, and care, you should be able to heal well enough to run again." She scanned the leg. "We're going to put it in a cast and a sling, so when it comes off in the end, you'll have to recondition those muscles. But yes, you'll walk and run again."

Sonja frowned. "How will you sling my leg? I don't understand."

Bethany bit her lip as she considered. "We'll either wrap it under your body like you're wearing a girth strap with the sling tied behind your withers. Or we'll loop the sling across your abdomen and around your waist above your withers. We'll just have to see which is most comfortable and stable."

The shouting behind her grew louder and Bethany grimaced. "Hold tight. Let me see if we can get these brutes out of here."

She stood and turned toward the arguing males. Corbin still tried to shove his way closer to Sonja, but Yarren, Idrissa and the other mares held him off.

"That's enough!" General Warrick's bellow silenced everyone into a gasping, angry stand-off. "You will all curb your aggressions until a decision has been reached."

"What decision is that, General?" Mack pushed between the mares, staring the larger man down.

"Whether or not to put Sonja down."

Bethany's gut sank, but her anger rose. "What's it gonna be, Captain Yarren? Step up to the plate, and be the stallion you claim is your right. Your mare needs protection and healing, and you can give it to her. So will you be the man you strive to be, or will you let your woman die for tradition?"

Yarren's gaze darted between her and Sonja, his lips pulled tight in indecision. Bethany's chest grew colder the longer he waited to answer.

"Can you heal her for certain, Mare Bethany?" Warrick rested a hand on Yarren's human shoulder. "Will she be fit to run again?"

"I can and she will." Bethany ignored Mack's groan as she met Warrick's gaze. "With proper care, food, and rest, Sonja will heal very well. She'll need the help of her stallion and her herdmates, but she'd recover fine."

Heartbeats passed as Warrick considered her words. Bethany hoped the weeks they'd spent negotiating had made their mark on the weight of her words. Because whatever he decided would set a precedent for how the centaurs treated their own people from this moment on. They'd have to see Sonja as a valuable member worth saving. *This could be the break Idrissa is looking for.*

"Very well, Mare Bethany. Practice your healing arts on Lead Mare Sonja, and her herdmates shall help her as she recovers."

A collective sigh ran through the centaurs around Bethany and she exhaled the breath she hadn't known she'd held. "Thank you, General."

"No! This is blasphemy." Stal Corbin shook in his rage. "She is changing everything."

"Perhaps this is a change more needed than a strict adherence to tradition, Stal Corbin." Idrissa squared off with the elder centaur, her eyes cold. "With Mare Bethany's knowledge, we will have fewer losses in our village. I don't see that as detrimental."

"No, of course you wouldn't, Lead Mare Idrissa." He scowled and turned to the side, snubbing her. "Mare Bethany has come and pushed you mares into thinking you should have more, be treated differently. But tradition stands for a reason and she cannot change it."

"No, it wasn't Mare Bethany who made us change, Stal Corbin. She only made us visible for the first time in hundreds of seasons." Idrissa stood her ground, though her voice didn't change pitch. "Mare Bethany has done nothing to this village that hasn't been coming for a while. She was asked to negotiate for awareness of the mares with the stallions. Just because you have chosen to ignore our complaints doesn't make it Mare Bethany's fault they're becoming visible. Change is here, and it's necessary."

"That's a lie."

"That's enough, Stal Corbin." Warrick crowded the

older centaur and herded him toward the doors of Yarren's barn. "I've made my decision and Lead Mare Idrissa is not at fault. I've heard your concerns and the council will speak of this after Sonja is seen to. For now, Mare Bethany will care for her and we will make our final judgment from the results of her actions."

Bethany breathed a sigh of relief when the doors closed behind the sputtering male and turned back to Sonja. The palomino centaur hissed as she lifted the leg. "I'm sorry, Sonja, but we're going to need to splint this until I get the materials to make a cast."

Captain Yarren knelt beside them, taking Sonja's hands despite the disapproval of the remaining elders. He glanced at Bethany, but smiled at Sonja.

"I'm here, Sunshine. Mare Bethany will make it better, and I'll protect you." He raised his gaze to his other two mares as they crowded behind the couch. "We'll all help you. Roanie, Tierna, and me. Don't fear." His voice dropped so low Bethany barely heard him as he pressed his forehead to Sonja's. "I love you, Sonja."

Bethany's throat closed and she had to study the broken leg to keep the tears from starting in her eyes. She had no idea the centaurs showed such emotion. The last three weeks had been full of anger, frustration, and vitriol, but love had been markedly absent. Yarren's subtle display made her yearn for silly things like friendly smiles and respect from the males of her own species. *Instead, I get Captain America and Daddy's sycophantic smarmers. Isn't there some middle ground?*

Mack touched her shoulder, breaking the moment. "What do you need to get started?"

Bethany took a deep breath and refocused. "First, I'll need a split tree branch about a foot in length and cloth cut in strips. We'll stabilize the leg until the plaster can be made."

Mack raised his eyebrows. "You know how to make

plaster?"

Bethany nodded. "Yeah, learned it in a homesteading class I took in college. It seemed like a fun elective."

"Damn." He grinned. "I didn't know you could take homesteading classes."

"You should get out more, Major."

She winked and he snorted, but he turned to Yarren. "Where can I find a hatchet, Captain? We'll need to make a splint."

Yarren narrowed his gaze as he rose. "Why would you do this, human?"

"The name's McMacken, and I'd do this to help your wife, Captain. Now, a hatchet?"

Yarren hesitated and Bethany laid a hand on his arm. "Please, Captain. It will help her until we can make a more permanent cast."

Yarren nodded. "Very well. Come with me, hu— McMacken."

Mack patted Bethany's shoulder before he followed the captain out of the barn. Idrissa took his place beside Sonja.

"We've casted limbs before, but never a leg."

"I thought you'd never done this before."

Idrissa grimaced. "We don't tell the stallions when something minor like an arm is broken. Building a cast for that is easy. This is something else entirely. Will this work?"

"Yes, it will." Bethany gave them a tight smile. "Here's what needs to happen, though. You'll have to rig a sling, around her withers and waist, and Sonja will have to keep off that leg."

"For how long?" Sonja's face creased with worry.

"Six weeks at least." Bethany patted her arm. "Don't worry. You're young and healthy. That will help in this situation." She turned back to Idrissa. "If you've cast other injuries, do you still have the supplies?"

Idrissa glanced at Warrick, but he spoke quietly with the

other elders. "It's not something we announce much to the stallions. They hold to the old ways, but we still have some of the linen strips and the ingredients for making casts. Not mixed together, but available."

Bethany exhaled with relief. "Very good. I can mix them if you'll bring them to me with the linens. We'll wrap her leg first, then put on the splint and cast."

Idrissa nodded and retreated past Warrick. They conferred for a moment before the Lead Mare left the room, passing Mack and Yarren on the way out. Mack gave Bethany an encouraging smile as he hefted two pieces of a split branch.

"This what you asked for?"

"It's perfect, thank you." She fitted the wood against Sonja's leg. "Now I just need the linen to wrap it before we cast it." She gave him a grateful smile. "Thanks very much, Mack."

His expression softened. "Hey, you're welcome, Bethany. We're all in this together."

Maybe, but him saying it made her heart warm just a little.

Sonja's amused grunt made Bethany switch her gaze to the mare as her face heated. Mack grinned and turned back to Yarrren, giving Bethany a little space.

"He's your stallion, isn't he?"

"What?" Bethany laughed with a shake of her head. "No. He's just a colleague. We aren't...mated or connected in that way."

Sonja tipped her head with a wry smile. "But you'd like to be, yes?"

Did she? Bethany focused on Sonja's white furred leg in her hands. "No, not really."

Sonja snorted and rolled her eyes. "I might not be your species, Mare Bethany, but I can read expression well enough. There is more than 'colleagues' between you."

Bethany opened her mouth to deny it, but Idrissa

returned with the supplies for the cast and Bethany focused on the task at hand. "Do we have any hot water going? We'll need it."

Idrissa nodded. "There's some started. I can get it."

Bethany stayed her with a hand on her arm. "No, send Captain Yarren with one of his other mares for it. We're going to have to straighten the leg and it's not going to be fun to watch."

She met Sonja's eyes and the mare swallowed hard, but nodded. Idrissa patted her shoulder then turned to the men.

"Captain, can you please get the kettle off my fire? We're in need of some hot water for this process. Take Roanie with you. She'll be able to show you where."

"But I must stay with Sonja." Yarren's eyes widened and unease slid across his features.

"Not for the moment. We'll keep her comfortable. Please bring us the water. That would help her most."

Yarren hesitated, his gaze jumping from Idrissa to Bethany and back. Bethany prayed he'd go because when she straightened Sonja's leg, she suspected the stallion would lose his military cool.

"Please, Captain. I'll have the materials mixed and I'll need the water. This will go faster if you could bring it." Bethany hoped her face showed nothing of her duplicity. He couldn't be in the room when Sonja screamed.

"Very well. Come with me, Roanie."

The red-headed mare followed her stallion out of the barn with a worried look over her shoulder. Bethany took a deep breath as the doors closed and Mack appeared at her side.

"What's going on?"

Bethany ignored him and met Sonja's gaze. "This is going to hurt like a sonuvabitch, Sonja, but we have to straighten the bone so it'll set right. Hear me?"

"Yes, Mare Bethany." Sonja took her own deep breath. "I'm ready."

"So, when I was growing up, we had these two huge hounds." Bethany smiled as she grasped Sonja's leg near the fetlock with one hand and near the knee with the other. "They were damn near taller than me and really slobbery. Most times I came in from playing with them and my clothes were sticky from dog slobber. My father would get furious because I'd ruined them."

Sonja laughed and some of her tension drained from her shoulders. Bethany nodded and jerked her leg straight, the bone snapping into position with a low crack. Sonja yelped and jerked, but Bethany held her leg steady.

"Sweet Goddess Epona." Tears leaked out of Sonja's eyes.

"Why didn't you warn her, Mare Bethany?" Idrissa demanded as she held the younger mare.

"I needed her relaxed or it would've hurt worse." Bethany slid her hands over the swollen leg. "I think it's straight now, though, so as soon as Yarren returns, we'll get started on wrapping this. Idrissa, take some of the linen and wrap a single layer around her leg, fairly tightly." She looked around for Mack. He stood beside Warrick and both wore their patented stoic-soldier expressions. "Major, can you help me with soaking the strips? I need to mix the ingredients for the plaster."

Everyone hopped to her orders and no one complained. Yarren and Roanie returned with the hot water and joined in without a fuss. Bethany mixed the clay and limestone powder, with a small measure of wood ashes, then added enough water to make a slurry.

"Are you sure you can do this?" Mack soaked the linen strips in the warm mixture. Their hands brushed each other as she continued to massage the slurry.

"I'm sure I can do it. I'm just hoping the mix is right and it'll set when it dries." She nodded to where Idrissa held Sonja while Yarren secured the splint to the injured mare's leg. "Don't mention it to the stallions, but the mares have set bones before. They should know the proportions more accurately than me. Ready?"

"Yeah, when you are."

Bethany nodded and brought the slurry to Sonja's side. "All right, folks. I need you to hold her leg straight, Captain, and I'll wrap the linens around it. Major, I'll need you and Roanie to smooth and pack the plaster around her leg." She met each person's eyes to emphasize her points. "I want you all to pay attention to how I do this so you can do it on your own if I'm not here. Ready?"

Everyone nodded and they jumped into motion. *Oh, I hope this works.* Especially since the tribunal hadn't reached its final decision yet.

CHAPTER TWELVE

Bethany stood outside Captain Yarren's barn with her head thrown back. Her shoulders, arms, and hands ached from the tension she'd carried throughout the day. Overhead, the stars of the Milky Way sparkled against the velvet black like glitter-strewn carpet. Bethany had once walked the red carpet at a Hollywood gala her father attended, but the noise and commotion had blotted out the joy. Tonight, silence reigned overhead as the crystalline stillness seeped into her bones.

She and Mack had worked into the early evening hours to make sure the cast on Sonja's leg had cured. The other mares had watched her every move, noting her technique. *I just hope I did it right.*

No one seemed unhappy with her efforts, though, and now she had a chance to relax. Yarren insisted she and Mack stay in his barn in case Sonja needed anything. Neither of them argued. *Anything is better than another night in the stockade.*

Bethany sighed and rolled her head on her shoulders, rubbing her neck with one sore hand.

"Stiff?" Mack's voice came out of the night silence and made her jump.

"Good heavens! Where did you come from?" She pressed a hand to her chest to stop her galloping heart.

Mack chuckled and held up his backpack. "Just visited the stockade for my gear. Wouldn't do to leave anything for the centaurs."

Bethany blinked as he wrapped his gear in his discarded pants. "How did you get in there without them seeing you?"

He tipped his head to look at her from the corner of his eyes. "I'm special forces. I have a few skills for getting into places undetected."

"So you're sneaky in general."

He snorted a laugh. "You could say that." He pointed to her shoulders. "Neck stiff?"

"Among other things. Hands stiff, shoulders tight, knees sore. It's like I'm getting old." She hunched her shoulders to stretch her tired muscles.

"Here." Mack set down his pack and stepped up behind her, resting his hands on the tight muscles in her shoulders. "Let me work on those a minute."

Strong callused thumbs dug into her muscles through her tunic and she damn near crumpled to his feet. "Oh, glory, that feels so good." Bethany closed her eyes and locked her knees as she gave into his touches.

"Damn, woman, are you carrying river cobbles up here? Feels like you have the trapezium of a gym rat."

"It's stress." Bethany groaned and tried to breathe through the fire burning her tense shoulders. "I carry it all in my neck and shoulders. It's been a rough three weeks."

Mack grunted and kept kneading her taut muscles. She idly wondered if his shoulders would be as tight. *Of course they are, but not from stress. I bet this guy could bench press a centaur mare.*

Mack's strong fingers worked their way down her back, massaging the muscles along her spine. Involuntary moans broke from her chest as the relief followed in the wake of his ministrations. He leaned close and the heat of his body warmed her through her clothes. The scents of the soap they'd used and his own natural spice flowed over her with the night breeze, and more of her tension blew away with it.

Bethany sighed and closed her eyes, relaxing into his his firm touches. She wished she could let everything go and hand it to someone else. Just have a moment of peace, even at home. *Home.* Where was that, now? The tribunal hadn't made their decision about her role in Mack's appearance, and there didn't seem much likelihood of getting back to their own world.

"What are you thinking of? Your shoulders tightened back up." Mack's voice washed over her with mild rebuke and she tried to relax again.

"Sorry. I'm wondering what tomorrow will bring."

"I've learned it's better to worry about that when it comes rather than speculating on trouble that may or may not exist." He redoubled his efforts on her muscles. "Besides, you don't know what the centaurs will decide about us staying here."

"That's my point, Major."

"Mack," he corrected, punctuated with a deeper rub on her shoulders.

"Fine, Mack. What are we going to do now?" She twisted her head around to look at him. "If they decide we have to leave the village, where are we supposed to go? We don't even know if we can go back home."

"I thought you didn't want to go home."

"I don't, at least, not to Kentucky." She grimaced. "But we're woefully ill-equipped to survive here without the centaurs' support. Back to our own world is preferable to that."

Mack's hands dropped to the outsides of her arms, squeezing gently. "We're not that ill-equipped. And you've made an impression on the centaurs. Look."

He turned her until she faced the village again, her view filled with the walkway to Idrissa's barn. Mack's arm pointed past her. She followed his aim and caught sight of two figures in the flickering torch light. Idrissa stood hand in hand with Warrick, their bodies relaxed and their gestures gentle. Bethany watched Idrissa laugh at something Warrick said and the general smiled.

"Wow. I don't think I've ever seen him smile like that."

"They look like a comfortable married couple." Mack's arms wrapped around Bethany's waist and she leaned into his warmth. "Wasn't that your job? To get the General back with his Lead Mare?"

Bethany nodded. "Kind of. Warrick said I had to convince his Lead Mare to tell him why she was giving him such a hard time. But when I talked to Idrissa, it turned out the problem was larger than just one stallion and his mares. It was more like they didn't think of the mares as equal members of the community, as centaurs they trusted and respected."

"They didn't trust the mares?"

Bethany frowned. "Not in the same terms as their brothers-in-arms. I was trying to get the stallions to see them as people—well, centaurs, regardless of them having breasts." She stopped with a frustrated shrug. "It's hard to explain."

Mack squeezed her. "You mean treating them as experts in what they do, regardless of their gender."

"Yes, that's it exactly." She glanced up at him. "How do you know that, being male?"

He chuckled. "My First Sergeant is a woman, but she has a wicked tongue, a brilliant mind, and she can kill faster than most other soldiers, no matter their gender." He looked sad for a moment. "She came through the portal with me, but once I got here, she was gone." He shrugged. "I actually hope she didn't make it through and is safe in our world."

"Do you really believe that?"

Mack grimaced. "I have to. Otherwise, I'd have to come back here once you're safe at home and track her down. I never leave a teammate behind."

"I haven't seen anyone else here, Mack." Bethany bit her bottom lip. "I hope she's okay."

"She'll be fine if she is here. Bryant can take care of herself and half a regiment all on her own. No one I trust more." He shook his head. "I'm holding out hope that she'll show up, either here or in our own world, calling me a fool for going it alone like some Hollywood hero." He gave her a brief smile. "There's no one better at doing this than Bryant, but being a human alone here is tricky. It's always better to have a team."

He played it off cool, but tension hummed through his arms. Bethany suspected he didn't like leaving any of his team on their own, regardless of their capabilities.

"Should I tell Warrick to keep an eye out?"

Mack hesitated as they watched the general follow the Lead Mare into her barn. "No, not yet. I don't want to get into more trouble with the news there might be another human lurking around. And they'd have to worry about Bryant. She's tough stuff."

"Tougher than you?"

Mack laughed. "Yeah, I think so." He squeezed Bethany again. "Let's see what tomorrow brings. We might have more and better intel in the morning."

Bethany sighed and nodded. "Let's hope so." She glanced at the barn behind them. "I should go in and check on Sonja. See if she needs anything."

Mack nodded and released her. Bethany missed his warmth immediately and rubbed her arms to reclaim a small hint of it. *What's wrong with me?* She had to admit Mack was turning out to be a surprisingly good companion and partner despite their short acquaintance. He at least could speak more than just the requisite grunts needed to make it through basic training in the military.

"Are you cold?" Mack reached down to grab his gear before he touched her elbow.

"Yeah, just missing your gigantothermy."

His laugh warmed her almost as well as his arms as he escorted her back into Yarren's barn. Sonja still rested on her couch, but her casted leg lay secured to her body with a sling across her equine chest and around her human waist. Yarren stood guard over her, his expression full of concern.

"How is she doing?" Bethany crouched in front of the couch, checking on the cast.

"She sleeps." Yarren scanned her face for a few moments. "Will she truly heal, Mare Bethany?"

"Yes, I promise she will, Captain. She's young and strong. It'll just take care and rest."

Sonja stirred at their voices and Bethany smiled apologetically. "Sorry. Didn't mean to wake you, Sonja."

"It's fine. I heard Stal Yarren's voice."

"I'm here, Sunshine. You just rest."

"Is everything all right? I'm not used to you being here."

Yarren grimaced. "I've been away too much. I shall change that, starting tonight."

"Speaking of tonight, where would you like me and the major to sleep? He and I will be taking shifts to check on Sonja." Bethany stood back to let Yarren closer to his mare.

Mack raised his eyebrows at that, but didn't contradict her as Yarren swung his gaze around the modestly furnished barn.

"They may rest on the old settee in the dressing stall. I believe it's large enough." Sonja gestured in the direction of a smaller three-walled room. "Thank you for staying with me, Mare Bethany."

Bethany smiled. "You're welcome. It's a far warmer place to sleep than in the stockade."

Sonja scowled. "How could they accuse you of endangering the village? You've been so helpful to the mares."

"Maybe I'm too much of a change to swallow." Bethany shrugged. "The problem is, I don't know where to go from here if they tell me I have to leave. I'm not from this world and the rift is closed." She grimaced. "Between a rock and a hard place."

"What about Cedarfell? Isn't there an older rift there, Stal Yarren?" Sonja yawned and her eyes drooped. "You used to tell stories about visiting there when you were a colt." She settled back against her cushions on her couch. "They could go through there."

A short silence followed as Sonja drifted back off to sleep. Hope warred with doubt in Bethany's chest and she looked up at Yarren for explanation.

"Is there really another rift, Captain?"

Yarren nodded slowly. "There is. A full day's ride from here. I haven't been there in decades. It was abandoned when I was a colt. I don't know if it ever opens." He shook his head. "I don't know who controls it now." He gave her a serious look. "And I don't know where it leads."

Bethany shot a look at Mack. "Do you think it's worth a try?"

"Are you ready to leave the centaurs, Mare Bethany?" Yarren's expression settled into impassiveness, but his fists clenched.

She sighed. "I don't know if I'll have the choice, Captain. The tribunal hasn't made their final decision. But if they say we have to go, that might be our best option."

"And if they say you can stay?" Yarren brushed some of Sonja's hair from her face. "Someone needs to care for Mare Sonja to be sure she heals."

"She will heal, Captain, and your other mares know how to help her and what to do. Trust them." Bethany threw Mack a significant look before she rose to her feet. "But if the elders say we can stay, then we'll reevaluate our choices." She waved toward the changing stall. "I'm going

143

to get settled in bed. I'll see you in the morning, Captain."

Mack held out his pack. "Would you take that with you? I'll be there in a moment."

Bethany nodded, too tired to argue. She just hoped she was the only one to see the glint of a gun barrel in the open zipper. Someone had thoughtfully left out some cushions and large blankets for the settee in the three-sided room and she stuffed the pack under the couch out of sight. Unfolding the blankets took the last of her energy and she settled down to sleep to the murmurs of the men in the other part of the room.

CHAPTER THIRTEEN

Morning dawned with an unusual sensation for Mack. Heat, softness, and the scents of apples and cinnamon in his nose. He opened his eyes to find Bethany's back against his chest, his arms wrapped tightly around her like he hugged a teddy bear. Comfort and contentment draped around him like thick blankets, and his recognition of them came only from their rarity in his life.

What made him so content now?

Bethany Stanton.

The truth rang in his head with an unusual clarity. He would've rested longer in that knowledge if his body hadn't warned him about his full bladder. *Talk about a mood-killer.* He gently unwound himself from around the sleeping woman and made his way out of the barn without waking anyone.

The morning shone clear with crystalline blue skies, but the wind held an autumn bite not present in the day before. It would be getting close to Halloween back home where everyone ran around in costumes and drank barrels of apple cider. Mack snorted to himself. In terms of costumes, the centaurs had everyone beat.

He finished with his business and took a moment to

evaluate his course of action for the coming days. His original mission of returning Bethany to her father in Kentucky seemed less and less likely, and not just because the portal at the archaeological site remained closed. His interaction with Stanton and Coolidge made it very clear they wanted Bethany back for whatever her presence could do for them. For her father, it boiled down to money. Mack suspected Coolidge concurred.

Bethany's more valued here with the centaurs.

The thought took him by surprise. He'd never questioned his mission before. Maybe the methods or orders as to how to carry it out, but not the mission itself. Now he wondered if completing this op really made sense. Of course he wanted to get back to their home world, but he no longer had the urge to return Bethany to her family. And she definitely didn't want to go.

Mack snorted. He wouldn't want to go back to that family, either. *The kicker is we don't even know if we can get back or where the Cedarfell portal leads.* They might be stuck in the centaur world. He shook his head as he made his way to the barn where his woman slept and stopped short just inside the doors.

My woman?

Mack had never been particularly possessive or romantic toward women. He'd spent most of his adult life in the military and the harsh reality often eclipsed any tender feelings beyond trust, honor, and brotherhood. He'd had short relationships, but his attention often drifted, too focused on whichever particular mission he had coming. Currently, the mission encompassed Bethany.

Movement caught his eye and he found Yarren bending down to tenderly kiss Sonja on the cheek. Mack had no doubt Yarren made a tough and capable fighter, knew how to lead, and took his responsibilities very seriously. To see him deliver tenderness to his lead mare struck Mack in the heart he didn't know he had.

I want that with Bethany.

The new thought astounded him and he stood gaping like a fool when Yarren stood up. The captain cocked his head and frowned a little.

"Good morning, Major. Are you well?"

Certain he looked like a gasping fish, he snapped his mouth shut and gave a tight smile. "Yeah, I'm good. Didn't mean to intrude. I was just thinking about doing some PT. Care to join me for a run, Captain?"

Yarren raised an eyebrow and snorted. "Do you think you could keep up with me, human?"

"At a jog? Yeah. At a flat-out run? Probably not." Mack grinned. "But I gotta get some running in. You got time, Captain?"

Yarren glanced at the stall they'd used before giving Mack a smile. "I have time."

Mack nodded as he continued to the stall. Bethany still slept and he crouched beside her, studying her. Even asleep, her face held beauty and life, something he'd missed for the last twenty years. Uncertainty welled up inside his gut and he rose to dress in his fatigues and boots. Someone had left them clean and folded beside their sleeping quarters. He settled them around his legs with a sense of rightness. The tunic he'd worn for the trial was decent enough, but nothing settled a man better than a pair of pants.

"Ready, Captain?"

"After you, Major."

Mack led the way and stopped to stretch out his muscles before the run. Getting older sucked and forgetting to stretch now came with a price. The captain watched him with amusement filling his face, but the centaur ran everywhere he went. *More than likely the bastard never pulls a muscle.*

Mack nodded to the captain and started off, heading out of the village into the plains around them. Running had always cleared Mack's mind of his worries, especially when pushing his body to keep a steady, fast pace. Yarren cantered steadily beside him and he let the world slip away from his awareness.

"Why did you come here, Major?" Yarren's voice intruded on Mack's zen moment and the big bastard didn't even sound winded.

"I was sent to rescue Bethany."

"By whom?"

"By her father." Mack didn't waste the breath to add his opinion of that action.

Yarren grunted. "Do you regret this?"

Did he? A few days ago he may have answered yes, but things had changed. Bethany wasn't a spoiled rich bitch without regard for those around her, and she hadn't run away like her father suggested. She had intelligence, tenacity, and compassion, qualities few in her circles at home possessed.

"No, I don't regret it, Captain. I only regret the lost members of my team."

Yarren grunted again. "There were more of you?"

"Yeah, there were supposed to be. Only two of us crossed the portal, but since I arrived I've seen no other humans beyond Bethany, so I don't know if my sergeant was kicked back to our world or made it here. I don't like not knowing what's happened."

"I'd wondered what kind of commander comes alone." Yarren jumped a small stream winding through the prairie. "I've seen no other humans besides you and Mare Bethany, either. I'll keep an eye out for them for you, but I think it wise not to inform the elders."

Surprise hit Mack as he stepped up his pace. "You won't mention it to them?"

"No. It's clear you're here for Mare Bethany, not to overwhelm our people. But I'm afraid the elders won't see it that way."

"Why are you doing this?"

Yarren shrugged his human shoulders. "You and Bethany helped my lead mare, Major. I'm indebted to you. If not for you, she would've been put down." His expression grew solemn. "She's my sunshine, my world. Without her, I'm lost. You and Mare Bethany saved me along with Sonja."

They lapsed into silence as they ran in a great arc around the village, but Mack's thoughts returned to the woman who'd changed more than just Yarren's world. She'd changed his, too, and he had a sneaking suspicion he'd be unable to let her go. *There's no way in hell she's marrying Coolidge.* Mack would face an entire cohort of angry centaurs before he'd let that happen.

But how would that affect Bryant and his team?

When they returned to the village, Mack still hadn't worked out how he would complete his mission, but he knew he'd never let Bethany go or walk away from her, even if they did get home.

"Good run, Major." Yarren clapped Mack gently on the back. "I'm impressed you can keep up."

Mack laughed. "Me, too, Captain. Thanks for the company."

"Anytime, Major."

He entered the barn and nodded to Sonja as he passed. The mare nodded back, but her expression tightened as if something had gone wrong. Unease settled into Mack's gut as he rounded the corner to their sleeping stall and found Bethany already dressed in her court clothes.

"Morning. Everything okay?"

She shrugged. "The tribunal has made their decision. We'll see what they have to say."

Mack's gut contracted a little, but he tilted his head and smiled nonchalantly. "I'm sure it'll be fine. This isn't your first rodeo."

Bethany coughed her laugh. "You know how ironic that

statement is given where we are? Can you imagine Warrick or Yarren in a Stetson and vest with a bandanna around their necks as they twirl a lariat over their heads?" She shook her head with a grin. "Gives a whole new meaning to horseman."

Mack matched her grin with a chuckle. "They'd make great cowboys and wranglers, though, wouldn't they?"

"Yeah, they wouldn't need a mount to chase after the steers, but cattle wrestling could be a bitch."

Mack snorted. "How do you know so much of rodeos when you live in the east?"

"One of the girls I went to school with was a rodeo queen and she showed me all the videos of her performing." Bethany shook her head with a whimsical smile. "She could really ride. She made the trainers from my father's stable look like sloppy amateurs for all they were "experts" in roping. Because of her I bought my first Western saddle and made my father buy me some of those sparkly western shirts."

"I bet he was thrilled about that."

Bethany shook her head before she braided her hair. "Oh, he was so happy about it, he made me go to a whole summer's worth of campaign parties. Not sure the shirts were worth it."

The memories seemed to steal her smile and Mack regretted reminding her. "Is it okay if I wear my own clothes this time? The tunic really does show a little too much leg, and I haven't reached my eccentric showgirl phase yet."

Bethany blinked before she burst out laughing. "Yes, I think you'll be fine in your fatigues."

"Good." He threw his shirt on over his head and reached for the vest. "Let's get this show on the road."

He followed Bethany out of their stall into the barn where Yarren stood beside Sonja, his expression solemn. Mack didn't like the tension in the air, but he shrugged his shoulders to loosen them and nodded to the centaurs.

Yarren nodded to the waiting guard. "The tribunal has decided."

Bethany nodded. "Yes. I'm on my way."

"I shall accompany you, Mare Bethany." Yarren squeezed Sonja's hand and headed toward the door. "Whatever they decide, I shall stand with you."

Bethany threw him a surprised smile. "You will? I thought you didn't care for me that much, Captain."

To Mack's surprise, Yarren shot her a half smile as they stepped out into the sunny day. "You grew on me."

Their levity faded as they followed the well-worn path to the Hall of Elders in the center of the village. Other centaurs paused on their daily tasks to watch them go by and Mack shook off the feeling of a funeral procession. Bethany took a deep breath as she reached the doors and Mack grasped her elbow.

"It's gonna be fine, Bethany."

She nodded sharply, but didn't smile as they entered the meeting hall. Warrick and the other elders stood at their usual places, most wearing stoic expressions. Only Stal Corbin had a look of expectation and triumph. *That's not a good thing.* Whatever had been decided pleased the Elder male far too much to bode well.

Captain Yarren ushered them into their defendant stalls and locked the gates behind them before taking his place to the side with Lead Mare Idrissa. Both shared the same tight expression and Mack belatedly realized they were mother and son. Idrissa nodded to the captain then turned her gaze back on her husband.

"Mare Bethany, this Tribunal has come to several decisions with regards to your behavior and presence in Forest Edge clan." The older Marine-like centaur spoke with sonorous tones, and Mack's dread deepened.

"On the count of reckless behavior to incite the mares to revolt, we find you not guilty."

Mack shot a glance at Bethany, but her expression remained serene.

"On the count of endangering the village through the willful communication and recruitment of another human, we find you not guilty."

A collective sigh echoed around them and Bethany's shoulders relaxed a little.

"However..."

However?

"While you have done nothing specific to endanger our village, your presence here has been deemed too disruptive and this tribunal has decided you are forthwith required to gather your belongings and your human companion, and vacate the village before the next sundown."

A stunned silence followed the Marine centaur's last statement, and Stal Corbin's lips curled into a malicious smile. It took almost a full minute before protests from Yarren and Lead Mare Idrissa erupted along with those of several other centaurs watching the proceedings. Mack blocked out the noise as he threw his mind into probable plans of action. They'd definitely have to try for the new portal now.

The cacophony built until Warrick bellowed for silence. "The decision has been made and Mare Bethany will leave the village by the end of the day."

"Why, General? What has she done to warrant such an action?" Idrissa stood with her hands on her hips.

"She hasn't done anything in specific, Lead Mare Idrissa, but her presence is a significant distraction and disruption to village life."

"She has *improved* things, General." Idrissa raised her chin. "She's brought forth long standing issues and made them visible. That it makes the stallions uncomfortable only shows what they have been ignoring. Mare Bethany is merely the catalyst to expose the problems facing this village."

"And those issues are now before us and able to be addressed." Warrick nodded as he crossed his arms over his chest. "But Mare Bethany's efforts are no longer needed, however grateful we are for her help in this matter."

"So you're turning her out? She's human, General." Idrissa advanced on the tribunal bench. "She has no specific knowledge of this world other than what she's experienced here. How will she defend herself against unknown enemies? How is this gratitude for her help?"

"You've overstepped your bounds, Lead Mare," Corbin sneered. "You see, General? This is why Mare Bethany must go as soon as possible. The mares believe themselves above us."

"That's ridiculous." Idrissa turned her ire on the malicious male. "You've done nothing but sow dissent and mistrust throughout Mare Bethany's stay in this village, Stal Corbin, and it's shameful. Your disregard for your own mares is your business, but as Lead Mare of this village, my rank affords me far more respect than you've offered me or any other mare. Have a care, Stal Corbin, your lack of manners is showing."

"You see?" Corbin whined. "This is why Mare Bethany must go."

Mack resisted the urge to grab one of the guards' knives and toss it at the elder centaur as Bethany raised her hand and waved it to get Warrick's attention. The room erupted into mutters and shouts, everyone overriding each other.

"Be quiet, everyone." Warrick's sharp order settled the room and he nodded at Bethany. "Mare Bethany, have you something to say?"

"Yes, General." Bethany drew herself up and for a moment, Mack saw her father standing there, dignity intact, and determination going strong. "I've heard your decision and thank you for coming to it in a timely manner. It's no secret I'd hoped to one day go home to my world, but my responsibilities in the village kept me here." She nodded at

Idrissa. "It has been an honor to work with you and your people to resolve some of the issues you face. I hope you will continue where I left off to find harmony in your village again."

Bethany shot a look at Mack. He gave her a short nod and she turned her attention back to the tribunal.

"However, Lead Mare Idrissa is correct. My knowledge of this world is limited, and Major McMacken and I would be better suited in our own world. Can anyone tell me if the rift in the forest is open again?"

The Marine centaur shook his head with a frown. "We have no information on that matter, Mare Bethany. The dryads have closed their borders to anyone outside their people for some reason. We can't get to the rift site to check."

General Warrick glanced at the older Marine centaur. "When did this happen?"

"Last night, General. The patrols reported the borders closed and rumors circulating something about a queen returning. They couldn't learn more."

"A queen?" the dark skinned centaur with dreds asked.

"That's what they said, Stal."

"So the rift in the forest is closed for more reasons than one." Bethany glanced at Yarren. "It's come to my attention that there may be another rift portal one day's ride to the west of the village." Muttering started and Corbin's smile faded. "While no one seems to know if it's active or even still there, I have no problem setting off for it as soon as I'm packed and ready to go. However, I don't know where it is or even in which western direction to go. I ask only that you provide me with some provisions and an escort to see me to my destination. After that, the escort is free to leave me and Major McMacken to our own devices."

"I volunteer my cohort to escort Mare Bethany and Major McMacken to the Cedarfell Rift, General." Yarren's voice rang clear in the silent barn.

"You, Captain?" Warrick frowned. "But you have an injured mare."

"I'm aware of that, General. But the one person know knows her injury best is Mare Bethany and I would be honored to serve as her guard on her journey from our keeping." Yarren's gaze never wavered from the General's. "I won't leave my mares unattended. Mare Sonja can come with us in the equipment wagons used for the cohort. My other mares can help with Mare Sonja's recovery as we travel, but it's only right to see Mare Bethany safely to her destination. I'm indebted to her for saving my lead mare."

"No, absolutely not. This is a breach in our defenses and a blatant disregard for protocols, General." Corbin waved a hand in protest.

Mack's tolerance for the whiny centaur elder had reached an all-time low. Yarren's hands tightened into fists with his own disgust, but his expression remained stoic.

"Some of those stallions have mares. They can't be asked to leave them on a fool's errand." Stal Corbin scowled at Yarren.

"I shall only ask those stallions who are currently unmated to accompany us, though I can't stop those who are mated from choosing to come with their mares as well." Yarren's voice remained steady. "This way should we not return, we leave no mares without care."

Mack studied the faces of the centaurs around him. All wore differing measures of disapproval, but only Warrick and Idrissa appeared more sorrowful than angry. *First time the kid wants to go out on his own, eh?*

Mack's parents hadn't been thrilled when he'd chosen the military over his geology degree, but they'd agreed the decision was his to make. Yarren appeared more than capable of taking care of his own herd. Mack shot a look at Bethany and the senator's daughter met his gaze with raised eyebrows and a short shake of her head. Yarren's decision appeared to be news to her as well.

"This is no time for hasty decisions based on misplaced gratitude." Stal Corbin crossed his arms over his chest while he looked to Warrick. "General, this young centaur has let base sentiment overrule his logic and perception. He's in no condition to lead or undertake such a journey."

Yarren snorted. "This wasn't a hasty decision, Stal. Mare Bethany and Major McMacken have earned my respect and I choose to help them in any way I can with regard to the tribunal's final decision."

"Captain Yarren isn't so young, Stal Corbin, and he already has three mares of his own." Warrick's voice held a note of anger. "You will refrain from your derisive comments for the rest of this trial. Perhaps learning some of this "base sentiment" as you so call it would be helpful to you in this."

As Corbin gaped, Warrick returned his attention to the captain. "If you've decided and are determined to see this through, Captain, you have leave to seek volunteers from the unmated in your cohort to accompany you, your mares, and the humans to Cedarfell."

"And if the mated men wish to come, General?"

Warrick grimaced. "I mislike endangering the mares, Captain."

Mack caught Bethany taking a deep breath and clenching her fists to keep from saying anything. Fortunately, the captain had more to say.

"I understand, General. However, the mares are more than capable of taking care of themselves and their stallions in times of travel and war, much like our more nomadic forebears. I believe in the abilities of the mares with their stallions. Epona forbid anyone gets between a mare and her foal. Even a stallion would think twice before trying that."

Mack shot a look at Bethany. While she didn't gape, she watched Yarren with an expression of admiration.

"I believe the stallions could benefit from the mares

attending them on this journey."

A period of silence followed Yarren's declaration, and Mack wondered if Bethany realized just how much she'd gotten the centaurs to change. Hell, most male humans couldn't handle having women in the ranks. This constituted a big step toward recognition of the mares as community members.

"Please give us a moment to confer, Captain."

Warrick turned aside and the other elders gathered around him in consultation. Mack watched them all closely. Corbin's arm motions and expression suggested he was against the mares being able to go, but the Marine-like centaur and the darker skinned centaur appeared more reasonable. The discussion grew heated until Warrick made a slashing motion with his hand and all talk ceased. They returned to their respective places at the bench.

"Very well, Captain. We have discussed it and if mated stallions wish to accompany you to Cedarfell, they will meet with no resistance from this council."

Yarren nodded and saluted the tribunal members. "Thank you, General. I shall inform the troops and make preparations at once."

"Captain." Warrick held up his hand and Yarren paused. "Come see me before you take final leave."

"Yes, sir."

"Very well. This tribunal is adjourned. The defendants are excused." Warrick rapped an old fashioned gavel on the tribunal bench and the guards unlocked the stall doors.

Mack waited for Warrick to walk away from the bench before he left his stall to stand beside Bethany. She gave him a brief, tight smile while the guards led them out of the barn and into the bright sunlight. Bethany took a deep breath and tipped her head back to stare into the sky.

"It's going to be okay, Bethany." Mack couldn't resist squeezing her elbow. "Hell, we even have an escort now. And the mares are being included."

She turned her solemn gaze on him. "I know, Mack, those are great things, but I'd just gotten used to being here. Now we have to find a new place and we don't know if we'll even be able to get home when we arrive in Cedarfell. What if the portal leads somewhere else?"

He didn't have any answers to her questions and she sighed, looking away. "Come on. We'd better help the mares pack."

CHAPTER FOURTEEN

It turned out they needed three wagons, but there were close to twenty willing soldiers from Yarren's cohort and a few of their mares able to pull them. Each wagon took four centaurs to haul their weight and the different members would trade off who tugged and who walked. Bethany rode in one wagon with Sonja while Mack accompanied one of the others to give the mare as much space as possible. They'd both offered to walk, but Yarren and the soldiers pointed out they couldn't keep up with only two legs.

Most of the village, including the rest of Yarren's mated cohort, gathered to see them off at midday. Warrick and Idrissa stood together, his arm around her waist, looking for all the world like parents watching their kid go off to college for the first time. Bethany had chuckled at the thought, remembering how she and her mother had been when her brother Kevin had joined the Navy. He'd been a tall, skinny kid with bright stars in his eyes. From the recent pictures she'd seen of him, he'd lost the stars and the skinny. His body had filled out and his gaze had become hard.

Sorrow stole her humor as she stared across the prairie splotched with cloud shadows. She missed Kevin and suspected he worried about her. She'd been gone nearly a month. *Sorry, Kev.* The wind kicked up a dust devil beyond the column of centaurs and she wrapped her robes closer around her as she sighed.

"He's not that far from you, Mare Bethany." Sonja nudged her with an elbow, grimacing as a particularly hard bounce rocked her body. "Only in the other wagon just there."

Bethany snorted and shook her head. "I wasn't thinking of the Major, Sonja. I was thinking of my brother."

Sonja tipped her head. "Were you close with this brother?"

"Yes. It was me and him against the world there for a while." Bethany took a deep breath of autumn-scented air. It smelled different on these plains than it did in her Kentucky woodlands. "Our dam died and our sire spent all his time securing his position in society, so we had to look to each other for support." She shook her head. "Now I'm here and I can't tell him where I am. I'm sure he's worried."

"It is often the way when family members leave the herd for unknown horizons." Sonja worked steadily on a hand loom, weaving what looked like a warm poncho-type garment in sunset colors. "When I left my village to mate with Captain Yarren, it was understood I wouldn't see my home herd again. It was a sad leave-taking, but I haven't regretted the choice."

"At least you had a choice. I stepped through a rift and no one in my family knew about it."

"I wouldn't say that." Sonja nodded her head toward the other wagon. "Your sire sent the major after you."

That's true. The question became, had dear Daddy mentioned it to Kevin? Given her father's proclivities for manipulation and secrecy, she suspected he hadn't said much. Besides, Kevin's position as a SEAL sniper didn't exactly give him the freedom to just up and leave to look for her. *Where's he gonna look? I'm out of his world.*

"Yes, he did." Bethany frowned. "Why would he send McMacken instead of my brother?"

"That's a very good question, Mare Bethany." Sonja gave her a secret smile. "Another good question is whether or not you regret it's him and not your brother."

Bethany opened her mouth to refute Sonja's statement, but nothing came out. She closed her mouth and stared out at the passing prairie, debating which man she'd rather see.

They still hadn't reached Cedarfell by the time the sun set, but the land had changed from grassy prairie to grasses with piñon and juniper trees dotting the landscape. Given how fast the centaurs could travel at a steady jog, even with loaded wagons, Bethany estimated they'd gone at least fifty miles.

Yarren called a halt and the soldiers set up camp. Mack jumped down to help them and Bethany admired him as he lent a hand setting up a cook fire and a tent. Sonja needed help disembarking from the wagon and she supported the mare as she awkwardly hobbled to the edge of camp for personal relief.

The evening had turned quiet with just a few sounds of night flying birds and the breeze through the juniper trees. Bethany found herself entranced by the open land marked by short, bushy trees. The scents in the air spoke of drier climates than she'd grown up with, and a desert sweetness she'd only experienced when her father had taken them to a ranch in Arizona.

The sun sank behind the hills in the west, painting the wispy clouds in pinks and oranges. The heat vanished from the air and Bethany shivered, rubbing her arms to chase away the chill.

"Cold?" Mack draped a thick shawl around her shoulders as he came up behind her.

"Yeah, a little. Thanks for this." She shot him a smile, admiring the last light of day highlighting his rugged face.

A three day beard framed his lips and jaw in short dark hair. "Looks like you're preparing for cool weather." She brushed his cheek with one hand.

"Yeah." He grinned and followed her hand with his over his face. "Haven't had much chance to shave."

"The camp more or less set up?" Bethany glanced back over her shoulder at the centaurs bustling around the fire.

"Yeah. The captain suggested we sleep in the wagon in case we have to make a quick break for it."

"Did he say why we'd need to take that precaution?"

Mack shook his head. "But whatever lives out here must run fast. He was adamant. Sonja will be in her wagon tonight, too."

"Good. She needs to be off the cold ground anyway." Bethany rubbed her arms again. "I'm glad I'm sleeping in a wagon with you."

Mack raised his eyebrows and heat suffused her cheeks. "I mean, because it's hotter with someone else under the blankets." That didn't help. "I mean, we'll stay warmer if we're together like that. Oh, hell, you know what I mean."

Mack laughed and Bethany dropped her face into her hands. *Could I sound any more inviting? Wanna have sex in the back of a wagon surrounded by centaurs? Jeez.*

He gently pried her hands off her face. "Yeah, I know what you mean. We'll both stay warmer if we share the wagon and the blankets since neither of us have cold-weather gear."

She nodded, grateful the darkness hid her embarrassment.

"Not that I wouldn't welcome the chance to see you without clothes. Oh, wait, I already have." His grin flashed as he released her hands.

"You're not going to see me without clothes tonight, mister. It's too damn cold outside to sleep anywhere near naked." She turned her back to him to hide her flaming face. "Though given the hair on your chest and belly, you could probably keep us both warm."

Mack's laugh rumbled through her back as he wrapped his arms around her waist. "So you *were* looking."

"Just because I didn't act like a twitterpated bimbo doesn't mean I didn't notice."

"I rather like that you're not a twitterpated bimbo. I would've been disappointed when I found you." He squeezed her gently and took a deep breath as if he wanted to say more.

"What?" One of her curses. Couldn't leave well-enough alone.

Mack remained quiet so long she thought he wouldn't answer. Bethany resigned herself to never knowing and tried to focus on the lovely cold evening growing darker by the moment. A nightjar called in the distance and its mate responded, their mournful cries making her want to snuggle closer to Mack.

"Bethany?"

"Yes?" She turned, meeting his gaze as he stared down at her.

"I wanted to tell you...how impressed I was with how you handled the trial. You didn't crumble at all in front of them."

Bethany got the impression that wasn't what he'd been about to say, but the compliment warmed her anyway. "Thanks. It comes from dealing with a father who's a lawyer and a senator. I got pretty good at hiding my thoughts from him."

"Still, what I mean to say is, that, well... Aw, hell."

To her great surprise, Mack dipped his head and kissed her, his lips warm and soft. Surprise mixed with immediate pleasure and she sighed into his kiss as he deepened it, brushing her lips with his tongue. She opened her mouth and her knees damn near folded as his hot tongue slid past hers in an erotic caress.

Glory be, he kisses like a dream.

Bethany wrapped her hands in his shirt and fell into his kiss. Hot arousal tightened her nipples and she resisted the urge to rub them against his chest. Mostly because her arms were in the way. *Yeah, that's my story and I'm stickin' to it.* Mack moaned into her mouth as her tongue tangled with his and it had to be the sexiest sound she'd heard in a long time.

He wrapped his arms around her waist and yanked her closer, the hard bulge between his legs pressing into her belly. She'd never really thought of a man's erection as sexy unless it lay outside his clothing, but the sensation of his hard flesh hiding on the other side of the fabric lit her fire and shortened her breath.

Mack must of have run out of breath, too, because he pulled back and panted hard while resting his forehead against hers.

"Sorry."

She gave a short laugh. "For what?"

"For taking instead of asking."

"You didn't take anything I didn't want to give, Mack."

"Thank you, ma'am. May I have another?"

Bethany laughed again. "Yes, sir."

"Oh, yeah..." His moan ended in a growl as he took her mouth again, this time swiping his tongue against hers with a more demanding thrust.

Bethany whimpered as his second kiss built her lust higher and her core melted with the heat he broadcast. When his hand burrowed into her hair, pulling gently, she thought she'd dissolve into a puddle at his feet. *More.* Her awareness focused down to Mack, his kiss, and the way his hands slid through her hair. It had been so long since she'd had a romantic encounter with someone who didn't want to impress her father, and she wanted to soak in it as long as possible.

She released his shirt and slid her hands down his body until they neared his belt. His belly contracted and he gasped as she tucked her fingers into his waistband.

"Oh, God, Bethany." Mack dropped kisses along her jaw beneath her ear and she swore she saw more stars than the heavens above her.

She'd almost gotten one whole hand into his pants when someone called her name from near the fire. They broke apart and stared at each other, their chests both heaving with the rush of adrenaline. Bethany scanned Mack's face for any regret, but he resembled a dark, mysterious warrior bent on taking what belonged to him. And in that moment, she did.

"Mare Bethany?"

"I have to go."

"Bethany, I—"

"I don't regret it, Mack." She smiled and patted his chest. "I only regret we have to stop."

He grunted with what sounded like rueful humor and ran a hand over his head. "Yeah, me too. Think we can resume after lights out?"

Bethany laughed with real joy. "I think that can be arranged."

"Hot damn."

She grinned and headed for camp, more excited than she'd been in years.

CHAPTER FIFTEEN

True to her word, Bethany had cuddled and kissed Mack in the wagon as everyone bedded down for the night. Mack hadn't enjoyed a make-out session so much since he'd been a teenager, and he'd fallen asleep downright giddy. And hard. The hard-on hadn't dissipated over the night and it made getting up a pain in the ass, but he regretted none of it.

His mind kept going back to the sexy moans and sighs she gave each time his hand coasted over her breasts or belly. It took all his considerable willpower to keep from ripping her clothes off and thrusting his aching cock into her. Still, the comfort and pleasure of simply holding her in his arms while they slept rejuvenated him and he'd helped Yarren and the other soldiers break camp with enthusiasm.

Bethany had helped the other mares tend to Sonja and they'd resumed their journey across the highlands. Yarren explained they'd be getting into higher elevations and cooler conditions as they approached Cedarfell. Mack tried to think about how he and Bethany would return to Kentucky and check in, but his mind kept getting stuck on Bethany. The sunlight burnishing her hair into gold or the sway in her hips when she walked totally derailed his thought train.

By late morning, his ass protested sitting on the hard wooden slats of the wagon and Mack almost asked to be let down to jog on his own. Yeah, the centaurs would leave him in the dust with how fast they moved, but at least he wouldn't feel like an unbalanced sack of potatoes to be hauled to market. He shot a look at Bethany in the other wagon and read similar misery in her body language.

Fortunately, Yarren signaled a halt at the edge of a new forest, the trees more evergreen than deciduous. Mack clambered down from the wagon and stretched out his disused muscles, noting the bite in the air though the sun shone down through the trees.

"Where are we, Captain?"

"Close to Cedarfell. This forest marks the last rise before the river valley. Can't you smell the water, Major?"

Mack inhaled, but his nose filled with scents of pine and sun-baked grasses. "How much longer do you estimate?"

"It's not far as the phoenix flies, but the safe path down into the valley is still a few more furloughs." He glanced up at the sun. "We're no more than an hour or two out."

"Good. I don't think my ass can take much more of that wagon."

Yarren snorted and gave him a wry look. "You could always volunteer to pull it, Major. I'm sure the men would welcome the respite."

Mack laughed. "Too bad I don't weigh twelve hundred pounds and have a horse's ass, too."

"Twelve-hundred and fifty, human. And not all of us have to have one to be one." Yarren tried for forbidding, but his grin ruined the effect.

"Shut up." Mack thumped Yarren on his equine shoulder with his fist and smirked. "I'd say Stal Corbin wins the competition in horse's-assery. Makes me look like a friggin' saint."

Yarren sobered. "Yes, that male wouldn't know

kindness if it bit him on the hindquarters."

"He's definitely got something against females of any species, that's for sure." Mack shook his head. "Whatever's wrong with him, thanks for escorting us out here. It's good to have a team again. Even if it's all twelve hundred and fifty pounds of it."

"You're welcome, Major. Mare Bethany saved my lead mare, and that more than makes up for any efforts on your behalf." He absently check the harnesses on all three wagons to be sure the leather held up. Mack followed him, grateful to stretch his legs while the others unpacked travel rations.

"Can I ask you a personal question, Captain?" Mack turned his gaze to the mares with Bethany's golden head shining between them.

"Certainly."

"Do you love your mares, all of them?"

"I find pleasure with all of them, if that's what you mean."

Mack shook his head as he checked over the gear on him. He'd chosen to leave his pistol wrapped in his pack in the wagon. "No, I mean more than just taking pleasure with them. I mean waking up in the morning grateful they're there and willing to do anything to secure their happiness for no other reason than their smiles. Know what I'm talking about?"

Yarren lapsed into silence as he patrolled the group, nodding and greeting the centaurs he passed. Mack strode with him, his attention split between where he walked and Bethany's location with the mares in the center of the group. The captain's silence turned thoughtful though his eyes kept scanning the surrounding area in search for predators.

"I can't say I truly understand what you mean, Major, but I will say this." He let his gaze drift back to Sonja and Bethany. "The thought of life without Sonja is enough to make me colicky and contemplate finding a good cliff to run off." Yarren returned his gaze to Mack. "That how you feel about Mare Bethany?"

Mack barked a startled laugh. "Yeah, actually, that's pretty close."

Yarren nodded. "You should handfast her and make her your lead mare before another stallion snaps her up."

Mack shrugged, nervous with the idea of handfasting. *That means marriage, doesn't it?* "I don't think I have to worry about it too much here. No other humans around, right?"

"Not that I've seen, Major. But are you willing to take the chance that something else might want her? When I first saw her I thought she might be a dryad."

"Those legendary tree people really exist?"

Yarren nodded as they returned to the women. "Look a lot like you except more...weathered."

Mack frowned. "Do you think the dryads could mistake a human for one of their kind, too?"

Yarren tipped his head. "I suppose it's possible, why?"

"Just wondering if my teammate really did come through the rift with me." The need to get back to the forest rose in him. "If the dryads control that area and they found her, it's possible they thought her one of their own and captured her. She'll need my help."

"What can you do, Major?" Yarren grasped his shoulder with a brotherly squeeze. "Not only is that forest a long day's ride away, but the dryads have closed their borders. Even if you could get back, you couldn't get through the trees. They have some sort of crisis they're dealing with and not even a centaur could get in. I will send one of my men back to the village and inform General Warrick of your soldier's possible presence among the dryads. But you're needed here with Mare Bethany."

Mack struggled to keep his voice even and his expression stoic. His responsibility had always been to his men, but he'd been sent in here for Bethany. As much as it sucked, First Sergeant Bryant would have to take care of herself now.

"You're right, Captain. I am needed here, but please do send one of the men back to inform General Warrick of my First Sergeant's possible location."

Yarren nodded. "Take heart, Major. It could be your First returned through the portal before the dryads discovered her and that's what set them off."

Mack suspected Circe's arrival sparked the tightened borders rather than her departure, but he nodded and went to check on Bethany. Yarren called for the group to prepare to move out and the mares helped Sonja back into her wagon.

"Everything okay?" Bethany brushed his shoulder.

"Yeah, we're good. Almost there." Mack gave her a smile to reassure her. "How are you holding up?"

"My butt's tired of riding in the wagon and I'm ready to be done with this wagon train." She grimaced. "Think we'll actually get back to our world, Major?"

He shrugged. "I don't know. If the portal works like the one in the dryad forest, we should be able to get home. We'll just have to see."

"And when we get home, what then?"

"You mean about your father and Coolidge?" Bethany nodded. "Let's cross that bridge when it's time."

He nodded to her and headed for his own wagon as Yarren gave the order to move out. Mack hadn't really considered what would happen if they were successful this late in the game. *And then there's the question of love.* Yeah, that. If what Yarren had said was true, Mack had gone and fallen in love with the woman he meant to rescue. A woman who'd pretty much changed the social structure of another species and managed to survive without his rescue. Did he really want to sentence her to her father's manipulations and embezzlement? What if Bethany never made it back home?

They don't deserve to find her.

The centaurs entered the trees and the wheels on the wagon rumbled a counterpoint to Mack's thoughts as they headed on toward Cedarfell. Could he complete his original mission when she clearly didn't want to go back to the life awaiting her? Mack's gut tightened. He didn't want to haul her back. It made him sick to his stomach.

Colicky and cliff-bound.

Yarren's words came back to him as Mack shifted his gaze toward the women. Hell, he didn't even know if they could get back. But he knew one thing for sure. He wanted more time with Bethany.

****

Bethany chewed the inside of her lip as they descended into the river valley through the forest. The path appeared little more than a break between the trees, and the wagons made the trip slow and treacherous. Her ass complained with each new bounce and she decided she'd had enough.

"I'm gonna walk."

"What?" Sonja looked decidedly green from the jouncing ride, but she had little choice.

"I'm gonna walk. Y'all aren't going fast enough to leave me behind and I can't take more of this ride." Bethany waited a few moments for the wagon to slow again then jumped over the side.

Her knees and ankles complained with the impact, but it felt good to stand on her own feet. Stretching her arms over her head, Bethany closed her eyes and inhaled the scents of sun-dried pine needles under the evergreen canopy.

"Mare Bethany, what are you doing?" Yarren thundered up, his expression a combination of surprise and disapproval.

Damn, don't these boys show anything else on their

faces?

"I'm going to walk. Y'all aren't moving that fast and I'll be able to keep up. My body can't take much more of the wagon."

He opened his mouth to protest, but she held up her hand. "Don't worry, Captain. I can follow the path and your hoof prints, not to mention the wheel tracks, without a problem."

"What's going on?" Mack appeared at her side.

"Mare Bethany's insisting on walking." Yarren scowled.

"Can't say I blame her." When the captain took a breath to protest, Mack patted his equine shoulder. "I'll walk with her and be sure she's safe. We'll be able to keep up with you and I can defend her if need-be."

"We'll keep up, Captain. And you're all around us. It's not like we're undefended." Bethany gestured to the other centaurs looking on.

Yarren huffed a sigh, but nodded. "Very well. Keep close, though. We don't know who all resides in these woods."

Mack scanned the woodlands around them. "Do you think the dryads live here?"

"No, it doesn't feel like one of their forests. Or if they did, they've moved on and left the trees to fend for themselves." Yarren fixed them with a stern glance. "But that's not necessarily the case with other residents."

"We'll keep up."

"Be sure you do." The roan centaur returned to the front of the cohort and motioned them forward.

"He's gotta learn to lighten up." Bethany followed after Sonja's wagon, easily keeping up with the halting progress.

"I suspect he's more worried about Sonja than the rest of us, but keeps an eye on everyone under his responsibility." Mack shrugged as he kept pace with her. "I'm no different with my team."

They descended down a gentle incline through the trees,

the scents and sounds of running water increasing as they rounded a gentle bend. Sunlight freckled the ground through the branches of the pines overhead, highlighting the few deciduous bushes in their gold and red glory. They finally broke out of the trees onto a mossy trail beside a rumbling river some twenty feet wide. Across the river the forest continued, but the trees stood wider apart and ferns and underbrush filled the ground below.

The centaurs turned to follow the river and the trail evened out. Despite the trees and rocks hemming the river, Bethany spotted structures up ahead where the valley opened up. White-barked trees grew around what appeared to be almost gothic stone walls with arched window and door openings. Flowering vines draped around columns leading up to the remnants of a one-story fortress with a domed roof.

"Whoa." Bethany felt her jaw drop. "Is that the portal?"

"That'd be my guess." Mack frowned as he paused. "Do you hear something?"

"No, why?" Bethany scanned the trees and path around them. Nothing seemed out of the ordinary. *If such a thing like ordinary exists here.* "What is it, Mack?"

He held up his hand as he jogged away toward Yarren. Bethany glanced over at the other women near Sonja's wagon and started toward them just as the musky scent of large mammal hit her nose. An angry squeal rent the air as a monster full of tusks and plate armor slammed into the middle wagon, shoving it and the two centaurs pulling it into the river.

More squeals hit Bethany's ears as four more of the huge creatures charged the cohort. *What the hell are those things?* Bethany ran toward the wagon with Sonja as the centaurs broke ranks and turned to face their attackers. She'd almost reached Roanie when Mack's body slammed into hers, taking her down to the mossy turf.

A grunting, snorting beast thundered by, skidding to a

stop just before the water. It turned and fixed its black beady eyes on her from a scarred and hairy face. Wicked tusks curling around its snout sliced the air as it swung its head from side to side, trying to get a better look her on the ground.

"Get up and out of the way, Bethany." Mack lurched to his feet and dragged her with him.

"What the hell is that thing?" She scrambled up with him, keeping an eye on the creature.

"An entelodont."

"A what?"

"An entelodont. An armored warthog on steroids." Mack dragged her back toward the female centaurs struggling to help Sonja out of the wagon. "They're straight out of the fossil record. The common name is Nightmare Boars."

"Holy shit."

"That's another way of looking at it, yeah." He shoved her close to Roanie's side. "Stay with the mares. They'll help protect you. And get Sonja out of the wagon. They're big targets for these bastards."

"What are you going to do, Mack?" Bethany gripped his arm.

"I'm going to get my Glock."

Her grip tightened. "You can't. A bullet that size will only piss the damn things off and make the others distrust us more. Please. We have to find a different way to defend ourselves."

An agonized scream jerked their attention toward the river. One of the centaurs still locked in the wagon harness fell silent as a boar trampled and gored his exposed belly. More shouts and battle cries filled the valley as the others gathered weapons to face their enemies.

"Get to the walls of the fortress, Bethany. Take the mares with you. You'll be safer there."

"Mack!" He ignored her call and headed into the fray.

"Come, Mare Bethany. Sonja needs our help to get to

174

safety." Tierna squeezed her elbow.

She growled under her breath about stupid soldiers and turned to the others. "Do you think the ruins are empty?"

"What choice do we have? Right now, we're exposed."

"Aw hell." Bethany focused on getting Sonja out of the wagon with Tierna's help while Roanie hefted a spear the length of Bethany's body with a blade as long as her forearm. Despite the gauzy-sleeved shirt the mare wore, she looked every inch a warrior in her own right.

Once Sonja stood on the ground, the four of them shifted closer to the ruins. Bethany's heart thundered in her chest as they worked their way through the melee. The boars' shoulders reached above her head and their malicious eyes gleamed with evil light. She'd always been creeped out by domesticated pigs at home. These hideous warthogs big enough to take out a car scared her stiff.

The scents of blood and pig-musk saturated the air and Bethany's eyes watered from the stench. She wiped them with her sleeve to clear her view, and ran straight into Sonja's flank.

"What's going on?"

They'd nearly reached the walls of the ruins, but in the doorway stood the largest boar yet. *Lord almighty, he's gotta be seven feet if he's an inch.* The tusks on the monster stretched almost a foot long and it wore enough scars to look like a bare-knuckle fighter after several bouts. It lowered its head and growled. The hairs on the back of Bethany's neck rose and she scanned the space around them in hopes of finding an escape route.

Trees. Get to the trees.

"I'm going to distract it so y'all can get Sonja into the ruins."

"No, Mare Bethany. You can't. You'll never outrun it." Roanie swung her body between Bethany and the boar.

"I don't have to outrun it. I just have to get up a tree." She inched her way around Sonja's hindquarters, keeping her gaze on the malignant boar. "Be ready to move."

"Bethany, please." Sonja tried to move, but her broken leg made her too slow. "You'll never make it."

Bethany shook her head. "Just get to safety, Sonja. I'm faster and stronger than I look." She nodded to them as the boar shifted in her direction. "Ready? Go!"

She took off across the open space, headed for the trees up the incline. An angry squeal followed her departure and the women shouted as the boar thundered after her. Bethany saved her attention for finding a tree she could climb. She had no hope of outrunning a thousand-pound pig bearing down on her, but she could out-climb one.

Her foot landed on a leaf-covered rock and slid to one side, making her slam her shoulder into the trunk of a nearby tree. Bethany staggered around with her momentum and the boar missed her by inches as it bolted past. Out of breath and smarting from the blow, she frantically looked for a tree large enough to hold her weight.

This isn't going as planned. The boar skidded to a stop and wrenched around, snorting with unbridled fury. *Aw, hell, here he comes again.*

Muscles protesting her quick movements, Bethany took off back toward the ruins, hoping she'd make it before the boar caught up to her. The decline gave her feet a little more speed along with her adrenaline spike as she pounded toward the stone walls.

"Bethany!"

Mack's voice penetrated her panic-addled brain and she glanced toward him as she ran. He hefted one of the big centaur spears and launched himself at the boar. Bethany screamed and ducked as Mack slammed the spear point into the beast's neck behind the head. Unfortunately, his momentum spun him in the direction of the boar's muzzle and the animal pivoted with an angry squeal, thrusting his tusks into Mack's side.

Mack went down beneath the huge pig's cloven feet and

screamed as it stepped on him. Bethany's answering scream made the boar turn back as she stood at the entrance of the ruins. She couldn't see much of Mack under the monster's body, but what she could see twisted at odd angles and was covered in crimson blood.

Fury unlike any she'd ever felt bloomed across her chest and she wished she could hurl it at the hideous creature standing over Mack.

"You misbegotten sonuvabitch!" The boar rumbled back at her and gathered itself for a new charge.

As much as she wanted to stand her ground, she knew she wouldn't have a chance if it hit her. *Oh, God, Mack.* Tears gathered in her eyes, but she braced herself as the pig launched into motion.

Time slowed down and Bethany witnessed everything as if she studied a museum display. The nightmare boar's hooves dug into the turf as it pounded toward her and little tufts of dirt flew out from its sides. Needles from the nearby trees drifted in the blood-scented air, sparkling in the sunlight. A higher pitched battle cry swelled around her as two centaur women flew past, hurling spears. The twang of a bow string made her duck and a fletched shaft flew over her head toward the charging pig.

Bethany stood up and found the dead boar skidding to a stop no more than a foot from her toes. Two spears and three arrows sprouted from its sides and eyes like grotesque quills.

"Holy shit."

"Are you well, Mare Bethany?"

She looked up into the worried gaze of Roanie and time resumed its normal speed.

"I—I'm fine." She looked at the carcass in front of her and shuddered. "That was a close call."

"Too close." Sonja limped up to her, a bow still tight in her fist. "But you're well. Let's check on Major McMacken."

"Mack!" Bethany gasped as her memory returned. "Oh, lordy, Mack."

She ran around the dead pig and searched for the man she loved. *What? Loved? Can't be.* But her thoughts splintered when she discovered his bleeding and broken body in the moss beside the river. She bolted to his side, afraid of what she'd find, but more afraid of what she wouldn't.

"Mack! Oh, God, Mack." Tears threatened to cut off her view of him and she angrily dashed them from her eyes as she scanned his body.

One of his thighs bent at an odd angle, though no bones protruded through his clothing. *Please, God, let it be the same with his skin.* He didn't move and his eyes remained closed. She almost let out a wail of pure fury and anguish, but it died in her throat when she saw his chest rise and his Adam's apple bob in his neck.

"Mack?" Fear tightened her throat and she had to clear it. "Mack, please give me some sign you're with me."

He groaned and opened his eyes, but agonizing pain filled his expression and more tears threatened to cloud her vision.

"Sweet mercy, Mack. I think your leg's broken." It was nonsense, she understood, but talking helped keep the panic at bay. "Is anything else wrong? That's all I can see, though your side's bleeding."

"M-m-med...kit..." His voice came out no more than a croak.

"What?"

"In...wagon...backpack..."

It took her brain several seconds to translate that into action, but Bethany lurched to her feet and ran for the wagons. Carcasses of boars littered the ground, varying in size from the huge monster who'd come after her to piglets the size of dogs. The centaurs had sustained a few casualties and several minor injuries, but most helped clear the area of corpses. Bethany scrambled up onto the one wagon left intact and searched for Mack's pack.

Where is it, where is it, where is it? She scrabbled through the loose belongings until her hands closed around the nylon straps of his Army-issued field pack. She didn't bother to open it as she yanked it out and threw it over her shoulder. Her knees protested as she dropped to the ground, but she'd be damned before she'd let her own body stop her from helping Mack.

He's gonna be okay. Somehow we're gonna fix him up and he'll be okay. She ignored the worried voice warning he could have internal bleeding and other things she couldn't fix. *Shut up!*

She ran back through the other centaurs to Mack's side, damn near falling in her haste.

"I'm here, Mack. I got your pack. Just give me a moment."

Bethany ripped into the pockets, pulling out gear and MREs in ugly Army green. The medical kit sat wrapped in thick plastic inside a metal canister. She pulled it out and set it aside as something the same color of autumn leaves caught her eye.

"What's this?" She pulled out a brilliant rust-colored feather sparkling in the sunlight.

Gasps around her made her meet Sonja's gaze. "What?"

"That's a phoenix feather, Mare Bethany."

"Wait, what?" She twirled the feather in her fingers and it left a trail of golden sparks in the air. "Really?"

"Yes." Roanie peered at the long shaft in Bethany's hand. "That's good luck and very valuable."

"For what? It's just a feather." She almost cast it aside, but Sonja caught her arm.

"For healing and increased health." Sonja nodded to Mack. "If he had it, then it was meant to help him heal from this. You must unlock its gifts and use them on the Major."

"Me? What can I do? I don't know anything about unlocking gifts." Bethany clenched her fist around the feather. "I thought phoenix feathers only granted protection against magical attack."

Sonja nodded. "Yes, but a phoenix is a magical creature and you're a great healer, Mare Bethany. That takes magic, and phoenix feathers often grant extraordinary gifts to those who already have them." Sonja pushed Bethany's hand closer to Mack's broken leg. "Call on your gifts. Call on the phoenix feather and heal your male, Bethany."

She almost opened her mouth to whine she didn't know how, but that meant she'd given up, and Bethany would be damned before she refused to try. "Okay. Any suggestions on what I should do to bring out the magic of the feather?"

Silence filled the space around her.

"Come on, one of you must know someone who found one of these feathers before. That's where the stories have come from, right?"

Sonja shook her head. "We've all heard the stories, but none of us have met anyone who has found one."

Just great. Now what am I going to do?

Bethany took a deep breath to calm herself down and scrutinized the feather. Even in the afternoon light, little sparks floated off the fringes of the down like little comets, and comforting heat warmed her hand. *That's just from the sun, right?*

But as she watched, the sparks formed a pattern, like a comet's tail, and slowly revolved around her arm, winding their way toward her shoulder. The heat built along her forearm as if she'd dipped it in hot water, flowing across her shoulders and down the other arm to pool in her clenched fist.

"Whoa."

Her right hand glowed and when she opened it, a ball of light sat in her palm.

"That's it, Mare Bethany. Now use that light on the

Major."

Sonja's words didn't make much sense, but with nothing else to go on, Bethany skimmed her glowing hand over Mack's broken thigh. The heat and light shot out of her hand and enveloped his leg, making Mack flinch. A loud snap preceded his leg jerking back straight and Mack cried out. Bethany gasped in chagrin and tried to pull her hand back, but the trail of light held her hand flush to his thigh.

"I'm sorry, Mack. Just hold on." *Please let this work.* She had no idea what all was wrong with him, but if anything she did helped him, she'd continue to do it. *Because I love him.*

Bethany couldn't contain the flinch of surprise, but when it jerked Mack's leg as if attached to her hand, she focused her attention on letting the light finish its job. Instead of fading as she half-expected, the tendrils of orange, sparkly light wafted up Mack's body and wreathed his chest and belly. They immediately glowed brighter and Mack arched, shouting in wordless pain.

"Lordy, Mack. I'm so sorry." She wished she could stop hurting him, but the light wouldn't let her move her hand. The tendrils lit his body in scintillating lines, like something out of a sci-fi movie, and things moved under his clothes like he shifted shape.

At last, the light faded, pulling back into Bethany's hand until only a spot the size of a dime glowed in the center of her right palm. Mack lay on the ground panting with exertion and staring at her with wide eyes.

"Mack?"

"Yeah?"

"Are you all right?" She scanned his body, looking for any external damage. His side had stopped bleeding while the light ropes held him.

"Yeah, I think I am." He blinked at her a few times, his thoughts running through his eyes too fast for her to interpret. "What happened?"

"I—the boar hit you and stepped on you. And I got your backpack and found the phoenix feather, and—"

"Phoenix feather? Why didn't you grab the med kit?"

"The centaurs said it would help heal you and you were bleeding so badly, and your leg was broken, and..." She knew she was babbling, but she couldn't quite stop as the emotion poured out of her chest. "Oh, God, Mack. You were so badly hurt and I couldn't think of anything else to do. I was so afraid you'd die and leave me here. And I had to try."

She took a breath to say more, but her throat closed and the tears washed down her cheeks. Mack sat up and wrapped his arms around her, holding her as she crumbled into sobs. Murmurs and whispers floated around her, but they were overridden by the strong beat of Mack's heart beneath her ear.

"I've got you, Bethany. I'm still here and I won't leave you. Ever."

She tightened her arms around him and sobbed into his chest, relief and the remnants of her fear blending together in her tears. *I can't lose him. I won't. He's mine and I love him.*

No matter how crazy the words seemed, they rang true when she held them up to really consider them. She loved Major Stephen McMacken and that's all there was to it.

"I love you, Mack." There, she'd said it. And she didn't care who all heard her.

CHAPTER SIXTEEN

Wait, did she just say she loves me?

Mack swore he'd misheard Bethany, but his heart thundered and the unusual sensation of joy flooding through his chest belied the notion. He didn't move for a few moments, trying to be sure he hadn't actually died or had fallen asleep. He inhaled slowly, taking in the scents of Bethany's hair and churned earth from the battle as he listened to the voices of the centaurs evaluating the results of the battle. Bethany shifted in his arms, sending a spike of pain through his ribs, but it felt more like bruising than broken bones.

So, not dead.

Mack wasn't sure he could answer her, but she appeared to be satisfied with listening to his heartbeat and snuggling against him. God knew he enjoyed every moment of it. Hell, only her efforts made it possible for him to hold her at all. *Yeah, about that...*

"Tell me again what happened so I'm clear on everything. You said you used the phoenix feather to treat my injuries?"

Bethany pulled back to look into his face, wiping her tear-stained cheeks. "I just told you I loved you and you're worried about the phoenix feather?"

Chagrin tightened his gut and he coughed a rueful laugh. "Uh, yeah. You know us military types. Love isn't part of SOP, so our hearts are usually MIA, and we're gearing up for the situation to go FUBAR."

She blinked then laughed, which loosened his gut. "So is this a SNAFU for you?"

"No, SNAFUs I do pretty well, I'm with the SNAIFU after all." He winked then sobered and leaned his forehead against hers as he exhaled, praying his courage wouldn't be DOA. "I heard you and I'm grateful for your efforts with the feather. I just don't understand how it worked." He tipped his head back and kissed her forehead. "For the record, I love you, too, Beth."

The smile she gave him would've healed a lot of his injuries by itself, and she threw her arms around his neck in a tight hug. Mack reveled in the feeling of her breasts pressed against his chest, but his ribs protested and he still wanted to know how a feather could fix anything.

"Really?" She searched his face for reassurance.

"Yes, ma'am."

"Oh, thank God."

He laughed. "Why thank God?"

"I thought I'd gone and fallen for a guy who was just using me as a meal-ticket with my dad."

The idea made him scowl, but he'd met John Coolidge and doubted the man had a sincere bone in his body. "Fairly common in your world, are they?"

"Multiply like flies on manure, you might say." She grimaced. "I took a chance, but I'd hoped you wouldn't be another one."

"I swear to you, Bethany, I want nothing to do with your father or his machinations." He hoped his sincerity showed clearly. "Now, how did you heal my injuries with a feather?"

Bethany shrugged. "I don't know, really. The centaurs

said phoenix feathers are supposed to help with healing and I just had to unlock it to make it work." She held up the feather, the edges sparkling gently in the sunshine. "The sparks blended together like a light beam and flowed up one arm and down the other." She waved at his leg with the feather. "It wrapped around your leg and chest, and snapped everything back into place. It looked like it hurt."

He had a hazy memory of intense pain just before he'd opened his eyes, but nothing else remained clear after he charged the boar with the spear.

"I think it did, but I don't feel anything now except bruising to my ribs." He glanced down his body and found his clothing stiff with drying blood. "Damn, he must've gored me good."

"I didn't stop to look." Bethany grimaced as she plucked at his torn shirt. "This is going to need a good washing and mending."

Mack nodded and took a deep breath before he shifted to get up.

"Do you think your leg's okay? I don't know if you should get up yet."

"No better time to find out." He gathered his strength to move, testing his legs.

"But everything I've learned says keep the limb still and stabilized." Bethany scooted back to allow him room. "Are you all right?"

Mack hated to be fussed over, but she'd seen him go down under the boar and he couldn't snap at her for being concerned. He got his right leg under him and gingerly pushed up until the left leg straightened. He set his left foot on the ground and shifted his weight onto it. No pain greeted him and he let out the breath he hadn't known he'd been holding.

"Everything okay?" Bethany's expression remained tight.

"Yeah. I'm good." Mack straightened and stretched, but

only his ribs twinged with bruised pain. Everything else seemed functional. "You said all you did was use the phoenix feather?"

"Yeah. Amazing, isn't it?" She handed the feather to him, but something else glowed in her hand and he grasped it to get a better look.

"What's that?"

"I don't know." She shook her head. "It showed up after the feather did its thing. I expected it to fade, but it hasn't gone away." She scanned his body with her gaze, returning to his eyes when done. "You're sure you're okay?"

"Yeah, I'm sure."

"Mare Bethany, come quick!" Roanie's voice broke into their discussion and Bethany slipped away from him.

Mack followed after her as she trotted toward the riverbank, her hand still wrapped around the phoenix feather. The other centaurs had cleared away most of the pig carcasses to be butchered for meat, but several of the soldiers lay on the ground beside them, nursing injuries.

"Oh, lordy. This is bad."

Mack had to agree. Broken limbs and lacerations covered most of those men lying on the ground, but Yarren's second in command had been gored in the belly, and bled profusely. Roanie cradled the man's upper body, tears streaming down her face. Bethany knelt beside the downed centaur and surveyed the damage. Mack's gut sank. The wound sucked in and out with the horseman's breaths and if he didn't die from blood loss, infection would have its way.

"Can you help him, Mare Bethany?" Yarren's expression shifted into stony withdrawal, but Mack knew he ached for his friend.

"I don't know." She bit her lip and laid one hand on the centaur's side. He flinched under her touch and her shoulders slumped. "I don't think I can do anything for him."

"What about the phoenix feather?" Mack crouched beside her. "If we get him stitched up, will it help?"

She shrugged. "I don't know. I'm kinda out of my depth here. I can try." She held up the feather, but all the sparks had disappeared from the fringes. It sat inert in her hand, like an ordinary orangey-red feather. "The sparks are gone."

"What about that spot on your hand? Do you think it's the same energy from the feather?" Mack flipped over her palm. "It's still there and glowing."

"Maybe..." She took a deep breath and held her hand over the open wound in the centaur's gut.

Light flared from her hand to encompass her and the soldier. It grew so bright, Mack and the others had to shield their eyes from its brilliance. Heat bloomed along with the light and drove all the chill from the air. The scent of honeysuckle wrapped around them then vanished with a hiss of the wind.

When Mack opened his eyes, the centaur soldier had a healing, pink scar on his belly and all the minor injuries to the others around him had disappeared. Even Mack's ribs felt better.

"Whoa."

"Better?" Bethany's voice filled in the amazed silence and everyone nodded.

"Yes, thank you, Mare Bethany." The soldier sounded breathless, but he didn't appear to be at death's door.

"Good." She rose to her feet. "Let's see who else I can help."

Mack followed after her as she visited every injured centaur, branding each with her healing light. Mack stood with her and his heart expanded with every patient. He'd never given much thought to the medics in his unit other than requiring them to be competent, but watching Bethany make her rounds gave him a better appreciation of her calling. And he couldn't help but love her more than he already did.

The look the soldiers gave her bordered on reverence and it occurred to Mack he could lose her. Not to the centaurs, but to circumstance if they returned to their own world. He shot a look at the ruins around the site of the reputed portal and wondered if he truly wanted to take them home. *If it even leads there.*

At this distance it looked innocuous, but it represented change, and possibly loss.

CHAPTER SEVENTEEN

Bethany stood at the edge of the ruined temple and watched the river tumble by, flickering in the light of the lanterns and camp fires. Tents lined the flagstone avenue leading to the temple entrance, facing the river, and scents of cooking drifted in the breeze lifting her hair. Exhaustion and tension dragged at her body, but she counted it as a "good pain".

Calm came with the sunset, along with gentle amazement at her new-found abilities. She'd healed every wounded centaur in the cohort just by touching them. She still couldn't believe it. The phoenix feather's healing properties appeared to have been absorbed into her, and now everyone thought she could do miracles. Bethany wasn't so convinced about the miracles part, but she couldn't deny her abilities had increased. She'd tried with Sonja, but the light didn't respond to her leg. *Must be only in acute or dire situations.* Still, everyone seemed pleased.

Feels damn good to be needed and wanted.

Which brought her back to the situation at hand. She turned and looked into the darkened maw of the ruined temple. No light other than what the stars provided dared enter the arches, but energy pulsed inside, a gentle heartbeat surging and retreating through the doorway. *Which means we can probably go home.* Dread and sorrow filled her gut. She belonged in the other world with cell phones and social media and fossil-fueled vehicles. But somehow it just seemed like a lot of busy-ness with no real substance. Bethany turned her back on the portal and scanned the centaur camp. Here she felt needed, wanted, and useful. In Kentucky, she'd become nothing more than a pawn full of money for her father's political aspirations.

She wanted more. She wanted love, friendships, camaraderie, respect. She wanted everything her mother taught her and her father required she give without reciprocation. Watching the centaurs set up their camp and help each other, they had what she lacked in her life. And now they offered it to her because she'd earned their respect and friendship.

What had she earned from her father beyond derision?

Jerky motion followed by a groan caught her eye and Bethany jumped into motion to help Mack put out their bedrolls. He'd already managed the tent, but she suspected his ribs reminded him he'd only recently healed. *Thanks to me. What a weird thought.*

"Here, let me help you with that, Mack."

He grunted and shook his head, but handed her one of the bedrolls.

"How are you feeling?"

Mack grimaced. "Not bad, all things considered. Still got a tweak in my ribs along my back, but other than that, pretty damn good."

"Good."

"What about you? Ready to head back to our world tomorrow?" Mack stuffed the extra clothes he'd received from the centaurs into his pack as a pillow.

Bethany sighed and straightened her bedroll out though it already lay flat. "I don't know."

"You don't know?" Mack raised an eyebrow. "This is the whole reason we came all the way out here, isn't it?"

"Yeah, I know, Mack." She flopped down on the bedroll and wrapped her arms around her knees. "Why else would the centaurs make this journey and have to fight off the damn nightmare boars? But I've been thinkin' about what's at home and I think I prefer it here."

"Here." He stared at her, his expression bordering on amazed.

"Yeah." She sighed again and shook her head. "I know what you're thinking and it's no different than what I think of myself."

Mack tilted his head as he sat down beside her. "What am I thinking, then?"

"That I'm crazy to want to live in the centaur world when I'm human and the folks back home sent you to come find me."

He grunted. "Yep. Which got us both in trouble and on trial."

"I know."

Mack nodded. "What has changed about going home?"

Bethany rubbed her hands over her face. "I realized I have nothing waiting for me there except my daddy's machinations on my life and money. The only one who'd miss me is my brother, and he's so busy saving the world most of the time he doesn't remember I'm around. Or not." She shook her head. "Here I have friends, colleagues, and respect for my abilities. I have purpose other than being someone's arm ornament or personal financier." She met Mack's gaze. "Here I gain something—respect, honor, friendship. There, I would have to pay with my self-respect, my trust fund, hell even my independence." She bit her lip. "Does any of this make sense?"

Mack nodded and gave her a sympathetic smile. "And what would you have to pay to stay here?"

Bethany frowned. "What do you mean?"

"There are pros and cons to any decision. The cons are pretty big toward going home, at least from what you've listed. But what will you sacrifice if you don't go back to our world?"

"Pollution, war, and greed?"

Mack laughed. "I don't think you'll be free of those here, with the exception of pollution."

Bethany closed her mouth and let his words sink in. "I'd miss my brother and Killian, and I'd be able to save my horse from being auctioned off. Plus I'd fit in better there, since centaurs and phoenixes and satyrs are fictional in our world." She crossed her arms over her knees and dropped her chin on them. "But I get more respect here, helping the mythical, than I do among my own people. The only thing that would make it perfect is if Captain Yarren and his mares would stay here in Cedarfell. Then I'd have purpose, friends, and respect."

"The centaurs are what you like most about staying here?"

Bethany took a breath to answer, but paused as she scrutinized Mack's face. Something about his question suggested a simple, flippant answer would be wrong. He waited, giving her nothing to judge from, nothing to decipher his inner thoughts.

"Are you referring to you in my life?"

"Yes, ma'am. I am. I kinda figured since you told me you loved me, I'd be pretty important."

"Yes, you are very important. But I kinda figured you'd be with me no matter what choice we made about the portal."

"Taking me for granted already, are you?" He quirked an eyebrow.

"What? No. Not for granted...Well, maybe a little." She chewed on her lip. "What would you rather do? Go back to our world or stay here?"

Mack rubbed his chin with one thumb. "There are a lot

of sane, logical reasons to go back to our world. People who know us and recognize us without making a big deal about our species. I have a team of people requiring my leadership. Not to mention the brass. I also have my parents who'd worry about me, I suspect."

Bethany's gut sank. "Oh, yes. Your family would worry."

"But..." Mack draped his arms over his drawn-up knees. "I understand being useful. Yarren talked about making his own herd here to protect this portal and have it under centaur control. There's plenty of space for a new herd and centaur installation, and they're already adopting some of the newer ideas you've shown them."

"Wow. I made that much of an impact?"

Mack nodded. "Yeah, I think so. In fact, Yarren mentioned his hope that the portal wouldn't work so you'd stay here with Sonja and the other mares." Mack shot her a thoughtful look. "I think he was pretty impressed with what you did for his men and hoped you'd remain here as their corpsman."

Bethany blinked at him for a few moments, her thoughts swamped in surprise. Earning the respect of Captain Yarren, who'd thought of her as nothing but a nuisance when he first met her, floored her. She let her gaze settle on the figures of Roanie and Yarren speaking with Sonja near their fire. She'd have a place with them, based on her merits as a physician.

But no Mack.

Bethany returned her gaze to the major. "What about you?"

"What about me?"

"What will you do now? You can't go back to our world without me, but you can't let your family worry." She waved at the ruined temple. "We don't even know if the portal works, or where it leads if it does. And we don't know if we could get back to the centaurs if we do go through. Plus there's the time thing."

"Time thing?" Mack raised an eyebrow.

"Yeah. You said you'd only been here three days when you found me, but I'd been here three weeks." She shook her head. "How long after I went missing did you come after me?"

Mack frowned. "Three nights after you disappeared."

"So, we don't know if the rift works, if it leads to our world, or even if it leads to our time. What if it points to some time in the future? Could you deal with hover cars?"

Mack blinked then laughed. "Hell yeah, it would be pretty cool, actually." He sobered at her grimace. "It's true. We don't know any of those things." Mack nodded. "But here's the way I look at it. It's my job to keep you safe and escort you home." When she opened her mouth to protest, he held up a hand. "Wherever home may be. My place, my responsibility, has always been with you, Beth." He gave her a brief smile. "And now you have my heart as well. The way I figure it, where you go, I go, and that's where my duty lies."

"But the Army and Senator Stanton. Won't they be expecting you back, with me in tow like a good little girl?"

Mack snorted. "I don't think such a creature exists, at least not in you. You're an adult, Beth, and can make your own decisions. If your father can't see that, he's not as smart as he thinks he is."

"Oh, I'm sure of that." Bethany shook her head with a grimace. "He's convinced he's the most important thing out there next to the President, but he's plum stupid when it comes to family."

"Family, whichever form it takes, is everything." Mack tucked an errant strand of hair behind Bethany's ear. "Senator Stanton can't command my respect despite all his years in office. I knew that as soon as I met him. You, my courageous and strong doc, earned it the moment you stood up to General Warrick and basically held him to his own rules. Helluva impressive response."

Bethany snorted. "Thanks. I'm sure he didn't see it that way. I know Stal Corbin didn't."

"That man is a horse's ass, literally." Mack grinned when she laughed. "He didn't know a good thing when he saw it." He reached out and turned her face toward him. "But I do. Let me show you my love for you. Not all men are as stupid as your father and Corbin."

Kisses rained down over her face and neck, soft and insistent. For a military man used to violence and force, Mack possessed the gentleness of a poetic soul. *Must be the geologist in him.*

He pulled back to look at her as he undressed in the lantern light. Bethany shot a look at the tent flaps, but he'd closed them securely and she returned her gaze to him. Finely honed muscles cut glorious shadows as his scarred skin came into view. Despite the odd blemishes, Bethany counted him more beautiful for each one. They offered a written narrative of his experience and sacrifice. She couldn't stop her hands from tracing the undulating muscles of his back as he pulled off his boots and pants.

His appearance distracted so much it took her a few moments to remember intimacy became easier when all parties wore nothing. She sat up to open her tunic, but Mack turned and stilled her hands with a kiss to each palm. In the light of the lantern he had the look of a warrior god, a Spartan scarred with triumph and intensity. Bethany shivered at his glorious male beauty.

"That's my job, Beth. Are you cold?"

"No. What's your job?"

"To unwrap the gift of your love."

He pushed her onto her back and took his time opening the buttons on her tunic. His fingers traced sensuous lines over her collar bones and breasts, outlining each shape and contour. Pleasure bloomed in their wake as his gaze followed their motions, periodically jumping to meet hers.

"You're beautiful, Beth. I've wanted to do this since that night in the stockade."

His compliments filled her heart, but humor quirked her lips. "The stockade inspired this? I didn't know soaked flannel and denim equated alluring attire."

Mack chuckled, the laughter rippling through the furred muscles of his abdomen straight down to his hard erection lying against his belly. He didn't seem to mind his nakedness and she enjoyed the view.

"Only on you. You know us military types. We see beauty in everything and everywhere we can." He kissed the skin between her breasts as he peeled her tunic off her shoulders. "It helps mitigate the ugliness of violence and war necessary in my profession."

Bethany sat up and shucked her tunic then stroked the new, healing scars from the boar on his side. His pale eyes watched her while his penis flexed at her touches.

"You're beautiful, Mack." She met his gaze. "Not in the accepted fashion magazine or political sort of way, but in a masculine way that encompasses intelligence as well as your experience." She trailed her fingers over his small, flat nipples at the edges of his pectorals. Mack inhaled a short, sharp breath. "Will you let me show you your beauty by making love with you?"

One dark eyebrow rose. "You can show beauty through making love?"

"Lie back and I'll give it a try."

Bethany pulled off her pants as Mack settled onto his back. He watched her with a half smile as she crawled over him braced on all fours, and excited satisfaction settled into her gut.

"See here?" She pointed to his chest. "This is beautiful for its musculature and scars. And these." She slid her hand down to his thighs. "They remind me of all the comic book superheroes."

"Are you saying I have superhero thighs?"

She laughed. "It gives a whole new meaning to 'thunder thighs', doesn't it?"

He chuckled and reached to pull her up to his chest. She rested against him, pressing her breasts to the hair on his belly. "As long as it's something you like, I'm good with it."

"Oh, it's definitely something I like. Let me show you everything I like about you, Mack."

Bethany grinned then proceeded to show him all the ways she found him beautiful. From the broad strength of his shoulders and chest to the rippled glory of his belly and thighs. She caressed all the different muscle groups, using the knowledge she'd gained in comparative anatomy to bring him pleasure. She took great satisfaction in making him moan and twitch with her touches.

Her final gift before she climbed atop his straining erection was a thorough inspection of his penis and testicles with her tongue. Mack moaned and thrust his hips, his hands fisting in her hair as she brought him close to release. But she stopped just short of completion to settle the tip of his penis at her vagina.

"Do you want more, Mack?"

"Oh, hell, yeah, Beth. Ride me hard, sweetheart."

Bethany needed no other encouragement and slid onto him in one hard thrust. She held her breath and met his gaze. His expression hardened into masculine intensity, his eyes glowing with erotic focus as he gave her a half smile. Pleasure spread from her core throughout her body with his hot intrusion and she matched his smile. They rocked together in perfect sync and reached their orgasm at nearly the same moment. She toppled over the precipice of ecstasy understanding she'd found a man she wanted. Not for his money or his position, but for his very being, the person living inside the body she loved now. He was more than his physical attributes or accomplishments. Her soul recognized him as part of herself, and refused to let him go.

Coming down from the euphoric high, Bethany nestled against Mack's heaving chest and thanked whatever deity watched over her that he'd come after her in this world.

I'm lucky this time.

"I love you, Beth." Mack's voice held reverence and realization.

"I love you, too, Mack. Stay with me."

"Always." His arms tightened around her and they drifted off to sleep tangled together.

CHAPTER EIGHTEEN

Morning arrived with the deepest sense of satisfaction Mack had ever experienced. He lay undressed in a tent in an exotic land, but contentment filled his spirit. Bethany's warm, naked body snuggled against him and her soft breathing soothed away any discomfort. He wouldn't choose to be anywhere else. Home had become anywhere this woman existed.

The problems of the day knocked at the back door of his mind. He and Bethany still didn't know if the portal would work or if they would even get back to Kentucky, but Mack understood one thing for certain. He'd never let Bethany go. A woman of her caliber came to a man rarely, if ever. While he'd met one like her in Circe Bryant, they'd had nothing like the heart-connection he'd found with Beth. He respected and liked Circe, trusted her with his life, his team, and their success in missions. But Bethany had taken his soul along with everything else.

Bethany sighed and stretched, sliding her sexy limbs along his. His cock saluted the contact with a hearty flex, but Mack watched her wake with a combination of delight, excitement, and satisfaction. He wanted her, for sex, yes, but also for her company, humor, and resilience in the face of adversity. She embodied glorious fire when she stood up to the centaur elders over Sonja, and sexy as hell when she rode him to completion on his cock.

I want her, and not just for bedsport.

Bethany gave him a drowsy smile. "Good morning."

"Marry me."

She blinked a few times as her smile faded and Mack cursed his direct and abrupt delivery. *No hope for it now, just gotta ride it out.*

"Uh..."

"Not for money, or power, or prestige, but because you're the most remarkable woman I've ever met, and I love you."

Bethany scrutinized him with cautious stillness and panic welled up in his chest. What could he say to convince her?

"Let me share my gigantothermy with you forever."

Her expression cracked and she laughed, relieving some of the fear and tension in him.

"You sure know how to romance a girl, Major."

"I got skills." He gave her a cheeky grin.

She laughed again as he grasped her hand and squeezed gently.

"Please, marry me, Beth. No matter what happens with the portal, I want to be with you." He tried to put all the sincerity he could into his expression. *Not one of my best skills after being in the Army for ten years.* "Please be my lead mare."

Mack wished he had a ring or some other token of his promise to give her, but his proposal hadn't been planned. *Aw hell, let's be honest. I usually just wing it.*

Bethany tipped her head. "Lead mare?"

Mack grimaced. "Yeah, I'm not at the top of my game. It's early."

"I thought you military types were all morning people out of necessity."

"Yeah, well, everyone has an off day. This is apparently mine, around the most important question beyond what's for breakfast."

"Oh-ho-ho. I rank above breakfast at least." Her voice sounded wounded, but her expression filled with warm amusement. "I'm good with the lead mare bit as long as I'm your *only* mare. I won't tolerate a harem."

"So is that a yes?"

"Yes, I'll marry you, Major Stephen McMacken."

Jubilation shot through him and he grinned before he kissed her lips with all the joy he contained.

She laughed. "Shall we set a date?"

"Today?"

"What?"

"Yeah. I'm not leaving anything to chance. Whether we make it back to our world or even go at all, I want to know we're together in this whole adventure."

Bethany nodded with a smile. "That's fairly poetic for a soldier, Mack."

"Hey, I went to college." He took a deep breath. "I don't have a ring or the usual trappings of a wedding, but what's more important to me is the agreement and commitment between us. The rest is just window dressing."

"You know, women like a little window dressing."

Mack's gut sank, but he tried to shove it away. "Is it a deal-breaker?"

"No..." Bethany bit her lip. "But after today's adventure with the portal and everything, I'd like a party, a cake, and some kind of accessory to signify our agreement and commitment." She grasped his left hand and traced its lines. "It could be a ring, a necklace, or a tattoo, but I want something others can see. Is that fair?"

Mack smiled as all the concern drained away. He'd love to see her wearing nothing but the token of their connection. His cock saluted the idea, but he focused on her face to keep it from rising.

"Hell yeah. More than fair. It's a deal."

Bethany took his face between her hands and kissed him so sweetly. His cock suggested *now* was a good time to seal the deal, but voices from the camp waking to the day derailed that train of thought.

"Guess it's time to get up." Bethany gave him a rueful smile as she stroked his hard shaft. "Too bad it's not in this way. Can I take a rain check on this invitation?"

Mack snorted. "Yeah, for tonight."

"Deal."

They rose and dressed, taking their time by helping, or hindering, each other with kisses and caresses. Mack hadn't taken so long or had so much fun getting dressed in years. Still, watching the secret smile on Bethany's face as she braided her hair puffed up his chest with pride. He almost strutted out of the tent.

Bethany went to check on Sonja and Mack looked for Yarren. He found the captain overseeing the disposal and disbursal of pig meat. Yarren eyed his approach with a knowing smile and Mack wondered if his satisfaction sat written on his face.

"I see it was a good morning between you and Mare Bethany, Major." Yarren nodded with amusement. "This is good news."

"It was an even better night, Captain, but I won't bore you with the details."

Yarren chuckled. "I think I can surmise."

Mack snorted. "I'm sure. What I'd like to know is if you can officiate a wedding ceremony between me and Bethany."

Yarren's smile broadened. "You wish to make her your lead mare?"

Mack coughed, remembering Bethany's opinion on that. "My only mare. Humans are particular about that."

Yarren grunted. "I can officiate. When would you like to do this?"

"Today as soon as possible." At Yarren's raised eyebrows, Mack added, "Nothing elaborate, just an official promise before we try the portal."

Yarren's brows lowered. "So you've decided to leave us?"

Mack shook his head. "That's up to Bethany and she hasn't told me her decision. But my duty is to her, no matter what her choice is."

"That is a lot of responsibility for a female."

Mack shrugged away his irritation. "She has the most to lose or gain here. And she's more than capable of making decisions concerning her welfare."

Yarren shook his head. "You're truly smitten."

"Yep. Smitten with a capable and conscientious woman." Mack lifted his chin. "Can you do the ceremony after breakfast?"

Yarren nodded slowly. "It shall be done."

"Thank you, Captain."

"Can you convince her to stay, Major?"

Mack considered as he looked across the camp at Bethany working with the mares, weighing his own motivations with those of Yarren and his fiancée. His duty was to her, but he'd meant it when he said she had the capability to decide.

"I can add input and counsel, but ultimately the final decision is hers." Mack clapped a hand to Yarren's human shoulder. "If it makes you feel any better, I think she'd like to stay."

"I pray she does."

"We'll see."

$$****$$

The ceremony took place at the doorway of the ruined temple. Yarren looked huge surrounded by the cracked and weathered arch, but he asked for their promises in front of the gathered centaurs and the Goddess Epona. Bethany wore her most elaborate tunic and Sonja had woven golden, orange, and red leaves into her hair in a sort of crown. Mack stood before her dressed in his court tunic over his black cargo pants. Not the most elegant groom, but he could have worn nothing but his skivvies and she would've been happy.

I'm insane. I'm marrying a man I've known for little over a week.

She couldn't argue with the logic, but she also couldn't argue with her heart. It wanted Mack and now was her chance to keep him. Still, this was a big change and it had happened fast. Uncertainty and worry settled in Bethany's gut and she swallowed hard. *Dear Lord, what am I getting into?*

She must have looked panicked because Mack squeezed her hands.

"Are you all right, Beth?"

She met his gaze, the bright blue of Kentucky skies bringing reality closer than ever.

"I can't do this." She shook her head and shot a look at the centaurs gathered around her. "This is too much too soon."

"Can't do what? Easy, Beth. Calm down and tell me what's going on inside that head of yours." Mack squeezed her hands again, insisting she look at him.

"This. Marriage. We've known each other for just over a week." She swallowed hard. "What if you hate the way I leave my equipment everywhere or don't make the bed with hospital corners? Mack, I don't even know when your birthday is or what your favorite color is."

He smiled at her, but his eyes remained serious. "My birthday is June seventeenth and my favorite color is maroon. I don't need hospital corners and I'm sure we can find out how each of us feels about equipment."

"But what if love isn't enough, Mack? What if there are

just too many things about us that are incompatible?"

Mack took a deep breath. "We've been through some pretty stressful situations here, and we worked fairly well together. I don't think compatibility will be an issue. But I do think it comes down to being honest and willing to take the chance." He bit his lip and tipped his head. "I love you. There's no question in my mind on that or on marrying you. But if the idea of marriage scares you, maybe we should call this off." He looked like he'd rather face down an enemy with a howitzer than stop the wedding, but he raise his chin and gave her tight smile.

"It doesn't have to be so drastic, Mare Bethany." Sonja touched her shoulder and offered a gentle smile. "Perhaps you would prefer to hand-fast with Major McMacken, thereby giving you time to learn these things you wish to know."

"Hand-fast him? What's that?"

"It's an older tradition back before the herds had grown in size. Stallions would hand-fast with mares to find out if their union would make a strong Herd Stallion and Lead Mare." Sonja shot a look at Yarren and smiled. Yarren nodded. "I too wasn't convinced I should marry the captain, so we hand-fasted for the first year. It is a trial marriage that lasts a year and one day. For all intents and purposes, you will be married. But there is an understanding between all parties that should anything untoward happen, the contract can be nullified without hurt to either party."

"Can the hand-fast be made into a marriage before the year and day deadline?" Mack asked.

"Of course." Sonja nodded. "The year and a day duration allows the partners to learn how they behave in all seasons, no matter the weather. It can be made into an official marriage at any time."

Mack nodded and fixed his gaze on Bethany. "Does that work for you? I'm sure we're meant to be a couple and I love you, as I said. But if you're unsure, we can hand-fast, and you can try out my paces. You can take the reins on this because I know what I want, and it's you."

Bethany took a deep breath and tried to let the worry drift away from her. *What am I really afraid of?* Making an irreparable mistake. She'd seen her parents and their connection had been based on money and image. She knew less about Mack than anyone else, but he'd shown himself to be honest and honorable even in the short time she'd known him. Hand-fasting would allow her to get to know him better and yet keep their connection.

"Okay. I want to be with you, Mack, and learn about you. I'd be happy to hand-fast with you for a year and a day, because I love you and don't want to lose you or our connection." Bethany smiled and more of her concerns faded. "I, Bethany Anne Stanton, choose to hand-fast with you, Major Stephen..." She frowned when she realized she didn't know his middle name or even if he had one.

"Patrick." Mack winked.

"I choose to hand-fast with you, Major Stephen Patrick McMacken, for a period of a year and a day, whereupon we shall be legally and consensually married." The last word still made her heart rate go up. "What say you, Major?"

"I, Stephen Patrick McMacken, choose to hand-fast with you, Bethany Anne Stanton, for a period of a year and a day, whereupon we shall be legally and consensually married, till death do us part."

"Oh, yes, until then." Bethany grimaced.

"The agreement between Mare Bethany and Major McMacken is hereby witnessed, and all present shall verify that it was made under no duress or coercion." Yarren nodded to both and gave them a satisfied smile. "You are now hand-fasted."

"Do I get to kiss the bride at least?" Mack raised his eyebrows as he shrugged.

"Oh, yes, if you wish it. By all means, kiss your hand-fasted wife." Yarren grinned.

Bethany laughed until Mack stopped it with a sensual and tender kiss, swiping his tongue across her lips. Pleasure zinged down her body and curled her toes before he released her with the giddiest grin she'd ever seen on his face.

The centaurs around them cheered until Yarren waved for silence. Mack held one of her hands as they turned to see what the captain wanted to say.

"Now, as you are hand-fasted, and are meant to share your assets, Mare Bethany, there is a large portion of the boar meat set aside for you and your stallion for the winter months."

Mack snorted with amusement and Bethany grinned. "Thank you, Captain."

"However, we understand you're planning on trying this portal behind me in an attempt to return to your own world." Yarren's humor left his expression and seriousness replaced it. "While we may not have always understood each other or the ways of doing things particular to each other's species, we of the new Cedarfell Herd have grown fond of both you and Major McMacken, and would like to make a case for you to stay here with our herd."

Murmurs of assent filtered through the centaur crowd. Bethany swung her gaze around to Sonja and the other mares. Each nodded and smiled, hope filling their gazes. Bethany tried to smile back, but she hadn't decided what she wanted to do. Did she stay or did she investigate where the portal led? And if it led back to her world, would she be able to return here? Did she even want to take the chance?

"We'd offer you the position of..." Yarren paused and shot a look at Sonja.

"Master Healer," she said.

"Yes, Master Healer to the Cedarfell Herd. In exchange for this expertise, we offer living quarters, infirmary, weekly rations commensurate with your status as Master

Healer, and the protection of the herd." He took a breath, his shoulders tight with uncertainty. "Are these terms attractive to you, Mare Bethany?"

Bethany took another deep breath. She'd been offered a place in the herd, more than she'd ever been offered with her own family. Why would she throw that away for the dubious chance they'd be able to cross? The whole reason she'd come all this way was because she'd had no place in the Forest Edge clan, and the new portal back home had seemed the only option.

Now she had the option to live among the centaurs as their healer, valued for her skills and contributions, regardless of her gender. What more could she want? *Nothing.*

She scanned Mack's face, but he showed her nothing. What did he need? Would he be happy in the centaur world or did he need to return to the human world for his team?

"Mack?"

He shook his head. "The decision is yours."

"I know that. I need more information. Do you need to get back to our world to...I don't know, report or reassure your team, or something?"

He sighed and glanced down at his feet. "My mission was to get you home, but it seems to me you have a home and place here. I do need to contact my team, to let them know I've survived, but we don't know much about this portal. Where it leads, when it leads, or even if it goes back to our world. Is it worth the risk to find out?" He shook his head. "I don't know."

"You have to tell the Army. And your family." Bethany squared her shoulders. "And we're a couple now. Hell, you should probably at least tell your mother you're engaged. We'll go through together and see what happens." She looked up at Yarren. "I have to do this with Mack, but I truly want to stay here. If we can return, would you still welcome me then?"

Yarren stayed silent so long Bethany feared he'd deny her out of spite. But the big roan centaur sighed heavily and stepped out of the archway to the temple.

"You'll always be welcome here, Mare Bethany, if you should return."

"Are you going to stay in Cedarfell?" Bethany reached for Sonja, taking the centaur's hand. "Will you keep your herd here?"

Yarren nodded as he drew his lead mare away. "We'll be here."

Bethany took a deep breath. "Okay." She turned her gaze to Mack. "I'm ready when you are."

"Let me get my gear and we'll go."

Mack stepped to the side and the watching centaurs gave him room to grab his pack he'd left beside the ruin wall. When he returned with the pack over his shoulder, they joined hands and strode for the center of the temple. The energy crackled and tingled around her, lifting the ends of her hair. Mack shot her a look of trepidation before gamely stepping onward. Sparkles from the sunlight streaming in through the window slots filled the space with glowing light.

"Ready?" Mack squeezed her hand.

"Not remotely. You?"

"Nope. Let's do this."

She nodded and they stepped into the center of the light.

CHAPTER NINETEEN

Bethany threw a hand over her eyes to block the light, but it had already started to fade. She found herself standing on an old wooden plank floor surrounded by rough-hewn stone walls, her fingers still entwined with Mack's. From the angle of the sun it was still morning, but the landscape had changed. Instead of a deep river gorge with tumbled boulders and thick forest, open grasslands surrounded the building.

"Where are we?" She scanned the land outside the open window.

"I don't know. Let's go outside to see."

Mack pulled her with him toward the thick wooden door. It had been secured with a matching wooden plank set into wrought iron brackets. Mack lifted the plank and set it aside before he pulled the door open.

A sudden explosion of motion made them both jump as a herd of antelope bounded away from the banks of the river meandering across the land to their left. The wind whistled through the grasses as the herd stopped a few hundred yards from them, ears perked toward the humans invading their space. A dark smudge of trees bracketed their view ahead and to their right, broken only by an old, dusty pair of wheel ruts leading off into the distance. But neither the animals nor the forest stopped their breaths.

"Whoa, is that Devil's Tower?"

The old sculpted volcanic neck rose out of the forest with all the majesty of an emperor, presiding over the world with the serenity of a saint.

"Yep, that's Devil's Tower. We have to be in Wyoming." Mack scanned the rest of the world around them. "At least, some version of it if we're not back in our world."

"How would we know? I don't have a cell phone or radio."

Mack inhaled and searched the sky.

"What are you looking for?"

He pointed upward. "Contrails. See? There's enough moisture in the sky for them today. Didn't you notice there were none in the centaur world?"

Bethany shook her head. "I didn't, but I was more worried about the things on the ground than in the sky."

Mack chuckled. "Yeah, that makes sense." He glanced back the way they'd come. "Wow. That looks like an old homesteader's house."

Bethany turned with him to study the ruin. The construction was old, but sturdy and had weathered the elements very well. No glass filled the window wells, but the walls remained solid and the roof shingles appeared sound. White daisies and buttercups dotted the edges of the building, vying for space with the tall grasses. Despite the air of neglect, the house seemed in good shape.

"Do you think we're in the past of the U.S., the present we know, or the future, Mack?"

He shook his head. "I can't tell you the year, but it's definitely a warmer season than where the centaurs are. See the daisies and buttercups? Those are summer flowers."

Bethany bit her lip. "Do you think rift will work going back to the centaurs? And if it does, do you think the seasons will equalize and we'll zip forward to their summer?" She rubbed her forehead. "This is making my head hurt. How can this even be possible?"

"The only thing I can figure is we're looking at worm holes through time and space." Mack scanned the homestead and surrounding grounds. "The portal in Kentucky didn't seem to have a linear time interface, not if you'd been with the centaurs for three weeks while I came after you only three days later. Right now we don't have a reference point to see how far forward or back we've come with this portal."

"Well, we know the portal works to get home to this world at least." Bethany rubbed her hand over her clothes from their hand-fasting ceremony and sighed, enjoying the warm sun on her back. "I guess that means we have to reconnect with the world at large, right?"

Mack grunted. "Probably. But we need some intel before we make any announcements. If it's summer, it could mean some time has passed."

Bethany counted in her head. "About nine months?"

He shrugged. "Could be. Then we have to decide whether or not to stay here or go back."

"If we can go back."

"Right."

"What about your family and team, Mack? Don't you need to contact them?" Bethany ignored the aversion to contacting anyone.

"They can wait a little longer. What do you want to do?"

Bethany let her gaze slide over the landscape, taking in the herd of antelope grazing in the summer sunshine and the majestic tower of volcanic rock rising into the sky. She didn't want her father to know where she was or have any ability to get at her money. *Although, if nine months have passed, he may have declared me dead and taken it anyway.* But she also wanted to do something with her life and the centaurs of Cedarfell had given her the opportunity to do and be something amazing. If the portal remained stable between their worlds, she wanted to be with the centaurs.

"I want to be the Master Healer for the Cedarfell herd, Mack." She met his blue gaze with her head up and her shoulders back. "I love you and I'm hand-fasted to you, but I want to be something more than just a trophy or a cash cow. I'm good at what I do, even if I haven't finished my degree here, and I can help the centaurs. I want to go back to them."

"Let me see your hand." Mack reached for her.

"My hand? What for?"

He flipped her right palm upward and pointed at the glowing dot in the center. "It looks like you still have the power you got from the phoenix feather despite being in another world. Maybe you can use it here, too."

She looked at him a long time before she said anything. "Does this mean you want to stay here?"

Mack shook his head. "No, it means I think you should consider the idea that you can be in both worlds. But first, we have to see if we can cross back to Cedarfell." He grasped her hand in his and led her back into the house. He closed and barred the door after she stepped across the threshold. "Ready to try?"

"Yes."

"All right. Let's do it."

"Ow!" Bethany hissed as a splinter caught her hand from the wood door.

"What's wrong?" Mack paused with concern.

"Nothing. I just got a splinter. I'm okay." Blood dripped onto the floor at their feet and the energy in the room surged, making the hair on the back of her neck stand on end.

"Whoa." Mack raised his eyebrows before the power built more.

Light shifted and brightened as sparkles filled the air.

Bethany glanced at Mack with a grin and closed her eyes against the brilliant light as tingling filled her body. When she opened her eyes, they'd returned to the abandoned temple in Cedarfell and a cheer went up from the waiting centaurs.

"We made it home." She smiled and waved with her injured hand as she hugged Mack around the waist.

"Yep. A good place to be." Mack kissed her forehead and led her out to their new community.

EPILOGUE

Mack kicked his feet up on the porch railing of their little stone cabin and watched the antelope herd meander across the grass of his "front yard." *I think that bull has some new females this year.* Though still technically winter, the March sunshine offered a welcome respite from the bitter cold, and Mack relaxed in it.

Six months had passed since they'd returned to their world from Cedarfell. In that time, Bethany had secured her trust fund, bought the land around the homestead, and created the Sagittarius Wildlife Sanctuary on a hundred acres to the west of Devil's Tower, Wyoming. Mack still chuckled at the name. She said she wanted to honor the centaurs who'd brought her here.

Mack hadn't argued. The portal remained remarkably stable and they'd chosen to secure it from random people wandering across. Since building the fence around the land, they'd left it alone for the plants and animals to come and go as they saw fit. Mack liked the peace and the silence of the natural world. It became a quiet sanctuary when he needed to think.

"Regretting your decision to retire?" Bethany pulled the

door closed against the cold air and handed him a steaming mug of coffee.

"From the Army or SNAIFU?"

"Both." Bethany sat down in the chair beside him and sipped her own coffee.

"Nah, not at all. I've served my time and seen enough weird." Mack snorted. "Although if you count living in two worlds at once, I guess I'm not exactly done with weird."

She laughed. "No, not exactly. I guess we could call this the new normal."

"Heh, yeah." He sat up and leaned over to kiss her cheek. "Just wanted to tell you I love you and to give you this." He reached down and picked up a bread-box sized parcel. "Happy birthday."

"Mack." She set her coffee cup down and grasped the box. "Thank you. How did you know today's the day?"

"I overheard the mares talking about it and headed to Sundance to pick something up for you." Satisfaction and pleasure at her curious smile filled his chest. When he'd heard the mares discussing Bethany's thirtieth birthday celebration, he'd ducked through the portal to find something to commemorate the event.

"What did you find?"

"You'll have to open it to see, Mrs. McMacken."

Bethany snorted at his name for her. She'd changed her name and all her legal documents to keep her father from finding her before she could use her money for what she wanted. Mack had checked the election results for Kentucky and Senator Stanton had lost his recent bid for the seat. Apparently his daughter's disappearance had adversely affected his reach despite the sympathy vote.

Good riddance to bad politicians.

"Oh, Mack, they're gorgeous." Bethany held up the pottery canisters printed with pine boughs and animal footprints in gray against a terra cotta background. Dark green glaze covered the rims and lids to the canisters.

"Wow. Looks like wolf, elk, and bobcat prints."

"Yep. I thought you could use them for your herbs and creams in the clinic."

"Yes, they'd be perfect for that. Thank you." She set the canisters down and straddled his lap, grinning with sultry joy. "I love them."

"Happy birthday, sweetheart." Mack kissed his wife with contentment.

The contentment disappeared as the sound of tires on the gravel driveway of the Sanctuary reached his ears. Bethany stiffened and scooted off his lap as he shifted forward to see who approached. The black Chevy pickup truck sped up the road, frightening the antelope herd into flight and kicking up dust. Mack scanned the vehicle as he rose, pushing Bethany behind him. Two people sat behind the bug splattered glass of the vehicle with California tags.

"You expecting a delivery of supplies today, Mack?"

"Not all the way from California." His gut tightened. Had the Army decided to track him down after his retirement?

The truck slid to a stop, spraying gravel and slushy snow to the foot of the porch. Mack rose to his feet and stood beside Bethany as they waited for the visitors to present themselves. A woman got out of the passenger side, her auburn hair woven into a braid from under her woolen beanie. She had freckles across her nose and a cautious smile.

The driver got out and strode around the front of the truck with an intensity Mack recognized from his experience in SpecOps. The man wore jeans and a heavy leather jacket, but his motions were controlled and graceful. He scanned the world around them, looking for hidden assailants before his gaze zeroed in on Bethany with intense focus

Sniper. Mack's gut tightened more.

"Bethany! Where the hell have you been for the last

eighteen months?" The demand accompanied a quiet, but hard voice and fisted hands at his sides.

The woman from the truck shot Mack an apologetic look as she smiled.

"And who are you?" Mack crossed his arms over his chest as he sidled closer to the rifle leaning against the porch railing.

"Chief Petty Officer Kevin Stanton. I'm Bethany's brother."

THE END

THE NAVY'S GHOST
SNEEK PEEK

A SEAL is strongest with her Team...

Ensign Christiana "Ghost" Brickman is the only female SEAL to survive BUD/S training, a real Navy Jane. But when an ambush ends her career as an active SEAL, she's free to pursue other interests. Like her two best friends Lt. Jim "Retro" Waters and Chief Warrant Officer Todd "Magic" Hunter. She's wanted them for over a year, but never dared to approach them while in the squad.

Retro has fought his dark desires since high school, certain the need to share a woman unnatural. Magic had never considered sharing before Ghost mentions it, but it solves his dilemma of choosing between his best friend and his woman. But Retro balks at Ghost's offer to share and retreats from both when she marries Magic.

Everyone feels Retro's loss, but he ignores the ache of their broken connection in favor of living 'normal.' When Ghost and the other wives of Beta Squad are kidnapped, Retro must reevaluate how much both Ghost and Magic mean to him. And he must decide how far he's willing to go to save the woman he loves, before she becomes the Navy's ghost.

OTHER BOOKS BY SIOBHAN MUIR

Her Devoted Vampire (from Evernight Publishing)
Queen Bitch of the Callowwood Pack (from Siren Publishing)
Not a Dragon's Standard Virgin (from Siren Publishing)

Cloudburst Colorado Series
A Hell Hound's Fire (from Three Lakes Books)
The Beltane Witch (from Three Lakes Books)

Christmas I.C.E. Magic (Happy Holidays from the Crescent Moon Lodge Anthology)
Cloudburst Ice Magic (from Three Lakes Books)

Bad Boys of Beta Squad Series
Bronco's Rough Ride (from Three Lakes Books)
The Navy's Ghost (from Three Lakes Books)

Coming Soon
A Centaur's Solstice Wish (Rifts #1.5)
Cloudburst Coffee & Spa (Cloudburst Colorado #3)
Second Chance Succubus

ABOUT THE AUTHOR

Siobhan Muir lives in Cheyenne, Wyoming, with her husband, two daughters, and a vegetarian cat she swears is a shape-shifter, though he's never shifted when she can see him. When not writing, she can be found looking down a microscope at fossil fox teeth, pursuing her other love, paleontology. An avid reader of science fiction/fantasy, her husband gave her a paranormal romance for Christmas one year, and she was hooked for good.

In previous lives, Siobhan has been an actor at the Colorado Renaissance Festival, a field geologist in the Aleutian Islands, and restored inter-planetary imagery at the USGS. She's hiked to the top of Mount St. Helens and to the bottom of Meteor Crater.

Siobhan writes kick-ass adventure with hot sex for men and women to enjoy. She believes in happily ever after, redemption, and communication, all of which you will find in her paranormal romance stories.

Connect with Siobhan online at:
http://siobhanmuir.com
http://www.facebook.com/siobhan.muir.35
http://www.tsu.co/SiobhanMuir
http://twitter.com/SiobhanMuir
http://siobhanmuir.blogspot.com
http://pinterest.com/siobhanmuir.35